Kendall's Deadly Match

by

Jerri Drennen

Redeeming the Reporter

The Wild Rose Press, Inc.
PO Box 708
Adams Basin, NY 14410-0708
Visit us at www.thewildrosepress.com

Publishing History
First Edition, 2025
Trade Paperback ISBN 978-1-5092-6102-4
Digital ISBN 978-1-5092-6103-1

Redeeming the Reporter
Published in the United States of America

Dedication

To all the ladies of my critique group who have helped me write through the darkest days of grief. They know who they are.

Chapter One

"How the hell did I get here?" Tate Donnelly asked himself for the umpteenth time that week, shaking his head in disgust. He had a Pulitzer for his investigative writing, the most prestigious award any journalist could receive, and yet now he was no better than a goddamned newspaper-boy.

Could things get any worse?

He sucked in a labored breath and glanced around the rundown cul-de-sac. The sun had started to rise, an orangish-yellow glow lighting up the sky to the east of town.

He'd arrived almost an hour ago and stood on the sidewalk, watching an officer stand guard outside the front door of a dirty-looking white home. An older model, light blue pickup sat derelict on cement blocks in the driveway, the yard filled with ugly ceramic gnomes and other assorted junk. This whole thing was probably a waste of time. No story at all, but he still had to be here, according to his editor, to find out for sure. Any police presence was followed up on by the local press. Tate, being low man on the totem pole, got all the early morning details.

He toed the right side of his shoe with his left, scraping a crust of dirt off the sole. Clearly, his days of glory were over, the *New York Times* job he'd worked so hard to get, now gone. All because of a chance encounter and indiscretion that forced him to leave Washington, D.C., faster than that political scandal trended on social media. He squeezed his eyes closed for a moment, then opened them again. His stupidity still sent him off the deep end.

At least, *The Gazette* in Kendall, Missouri had given him a fresh start in his field, if you could call covering corrupt school officials, petty theft, and whatever *this* was, actual journalism. On days like today, Tate wondered if it was even worth it.

He plunged a fist deep into his trouser pocket. The sooner he acclimated himself to this new lifestyle, the better off he'd be. After all, he couldn't change things. Hell, if he could, he'd have never stepped into that elevator that fateful day.

Loud, persistent barking grabbed his attention. Off to the side, a tiny slip of a girl being pulled by a large, shaggy dog was headed straight for him. "No, Princess. Slow down," she said, right as the dog yanked at the leash and broke free.

Tate took a step back, thinking the dog would simply pass. Instead, it barreled into him, its nose rooting right up into his crotch, sniffing and snorting as if it were a bull in a matador's arena.

"Jesus Christ." He tried to shove the dog's head away with little success. The beast was on a mission to castrate him.

"You're being bad, Princess," the girl scolded.

Being bad. Who was she kidding? The dog was slobbering all over the front of his slacks. And the kicker? The assault on his manhood, the laving attention to his family jewels, was the most action he'd seen since his fall from grace. Eight months ago and counting.

2

Tate shook the memory off and once again shoved the dog's head away.

The girl grabbed the leash and tugged at the animal, finally getting her to back away from his most prized possession. Well, maybe not so prized since it had gotten him here in the first place.

"I'm so sorry," she said, looking up at him.

He noticed then she was no girl at all, but a full-fledged woman with the bluest eyes he'd ever seen, on a face that was wholesome and intriguing with a speckling of tiny freckles that swept across the bridge of her nose and cheekbones. Her hair was tucked under a Chicago Cubs ball cap, but her sprint to catch the dog had allowed strands to escape from beneath, revealing long, bouncy auburn curls.

She'd looked tiny from afar, but she reached the top of his nose, and he was tall at six-three.

She cleared her throat.

He was staring. *Shit.* He quickly glanced at the dog, whose tongue was hanging out the side of its mouth. *Sure, appears innocent now.* But looks could be deceiving. Maybe he should have the thing brought up on sexual assault charges. "You need to put a bridle on that thing or keep it corralled," he said, deadpan.

Her apologetic expression vanished, and those intense blue eyes narrowed. "She got away from me. I'm sorry. Send me the dry-cleaning bill for your slacks. I'll gladly pay for them to be laundered."

Tate gritted his teeth and refrained from rolling his eyes. The *corralling* comment had been meant as a joke, yet apparently hadn't come off as such.

"Don't worry about it."

"No. I insist." She reached inside her windbreaker

3

and handed him a card. "That has my number and address on it. Again, I'm truly sorry." She glanced at the officer, who had been watching them and wore an irritating smirk.

"What's going on, John?" Her attention now was focused on the house.

The officer sobered and shook his head. "I can't say."

"What? Why not?" She tightened up on the dog's leash when the creature started to move toward Tate again.

The animal clearly had an affection for a part of him.

"Sheriff said to keep my mouth zipped this time."

She frowned, then shrugged and turned to leave, giving Tate one last look of indifference.

"Nice to meet you, too," he said, glancing down at the card she'd given him. Carrie Pruitt. Grooming and Dog Sitting Services was in gold print. Were there even enough animals in town needing to be groomed and babysat for her to make a living? Then again, after his run-in with that beast, Ms. Pruitt didn't seem all that good at the job.

A clink of a screen door opening had him turning back to the house where a large, heavyset man in a tan shirt and pants stepped outside. Which had to be the sheriff.

Tate walked up the sidewalk toward him. He needed to get a comment, or he'd be toast. "Can you give me any information on the victim in the home and the circumstances surrounding their death?"

The sheriff cleared his throat. "All I can tell you is that we were called to the scene after a family member entered the residence and found their relative dead.

Additional details will be forthcoming."

"Do you have a name? Did they die of natural causes?"

The older man removed his hat and scratched at his balding head. "No, and no comment."

Great. All this waiting and that's all Tate got for his trouble. How could he possibly write a story without even the name of the victim? Then again, it probably wasn't a story at all. One for the Obits perhaps.

Tate glanced around. People had ventured onto their front lawns to see what was going on. He could ask one of them. Surely, they knew who owned the house since the police were being so tight-lipped.

"All right. Thanks *for nothing.*"

"I aim to please. Oh, hey, before you go checking with the neighbors, you might want to get a change of pants there." The sheriff pointed to Tate's crotch and raised an eyebrow. "People might think you have a finicky bladder or something worse and be nervous to talk to you. Then again, if you do have an issue, Doc Havers can help with that. He's just off Main Street, and welcomes walk-ins."

Tate studied the man's face. *Was he being serious?* Nothing in his features gave him away. Then again, the residents here were strange.

The officer who'd been standing guard snickered and slapped at his leg.

Tate sighed. Okay, so it was a joke. He should have picked up on it.

"Will do." Tate headed for his Jeep, planning to do what the sheriff suggested—go home and change. He'd come back later and talk to a few of the owner's closest neighbors. Because, if he wanted his D.C. gig back

5

someday, he'd have to rise up from the ashes here in this godforsaken place, a realization that made him want to lose the half a cup of toxic sludge the local café considered coffee that now sat like a mooring anchor in his gut.

His own stupidity had gotten him here, he was going to have to use his ingenuity to get himself out.

****

At home and with Princess kenneled, Carrie squeezed her eyes closed for a moment, feeling relieved. She still couldn't believe what had happened earlier with the tall stranger. The dog's escape was her fault—a first since she'd opened her business. She'd sprained her wrist last night tripping up a flight of stairs trying to avoid Molly, her Bichon Frise, who'd cut in front of her.

Please don't be fractured. She could barely feed herself right now, let alone pay a doctor's bill. Business had been slow because Doug Walsh was spreading rumors about her and apparently, his word had hit pay dirt. *Asshole.*

She drew in a calming breath and placed her hand around the now throbbing wrist. That morning, before she'd walked Princess, she'd wrapped it tight, thinking it'd be enough to handle the dog on the short trip around the block. Yet, when Princess had spotted the stranger and yanked at the rope, Carrie had lost her grip. She'd watched in horror as the Great Pyrenees attacked the man's crotch.

Once she'd reached the dog, she found it hard not to stare at the man's impressive-looking package. Not that she'd seen all that many in her twenty-seven years of life. Pickings were slim in Kendall. But *it* was eye-catching for a small-town girl like herself who didn't get out much.

When she'd finally looked up and saw him staring, her face felt like someone had turned the heat up one-hundred-fifty degrees. Thank God he hadn't seemed to catch on to where her attention had been and glanced at the dog. That's when she got a view of a full head of wavy, pitch-black hair—the kind you could spend hours running your hands through.

Oh, dear God, Carrie. When have you ever run a hand through a man's hair? Never. Not once. Ever. Besides, the guy's a jerk. He wouldn't deserve that kind of lavished attention.

Good looking though. His eyes large and compelling, the color of fresh-cut grass, highlighted by that dark, *finger-running* hair and sooty lashes longer than her own. Strong, kissable lips that…

OMG, enough!

Carrie rolled her eyes and continued to scold herself over and over until she had her thoughts under control. She'd been spending entirely too much time with animals and not enough trying to have a life. And clearly, the books she'd been reading were messing with her head. *Romance.* Men with thick, dark hair and hot bods. Heroes who save the female characters from the nightmares they've been living. Carrie doubted the sexy stranger would lift a finger to help her out, and frankly, she didn't need him to. She could take care of herself. After all, she'd been doing so since she came to Kendall over ten years ago. Since then, hard times had come and gone. She'd get through this as she always had—on her own.

She pushed the negativity away and stepped over to her stove to put on the kettle. All her friends had fancy single-serve coffeemakers. She could only afford instant coffee, and she had to hurry and drink it. Princess needed a bath before the Nelsons came to pick her up and with her long, thick fur, it'd take two hours to dry.

A few minutes later, the kettle whistled, and she scooped a couple spoonful's of crystals into her 'Dogs are Life' mug and topped it with water, stirring until the coffee was mixed. She then carried the cup through the rear entrance and stepped out to her garage where her grooming area and supplies were kept. She always set up everything in advance before retrieving the dog, and after her encounter this morning, she was going to need to be extremely careful not to lose control of the animal again.

Carrie grabbed three towels, her Oatmeal Lavender shampoo, and the nail clippers.

She filled the tub sitting about a foot off the floor. With her sore wrist, it would be a struggle to get Princess inside.

When the basin was filled, she turned to fetch Princess and gasped, her heart beating wildly at the sight of the one man she never wanted to see again. *Doug Walsh.* "What are you doing here?" she asked, looking for a way to get past him and outside. *Shit.* He completely blocked the door with his six-foot-one, two-hundred-thirty-pound frame clad in a pair of dirty blue jeans and a red flannel shirt with a ripped pocket. Carrie wasn't getting out without a fight, and she was sure that's why he'd stood there—to intimidate her.

He re-adjusted the frayed cap on his head. "No, nice to see you, Doug? How are you doing today?"

Big bobblehead with no brain. The man had been after her for six of the ten years she'd lived here and

8

never gave up no matter how many rejections he got. Carrie was sick of his harassment, especially when he had a girlfriend.

"I have work to do. Did you want something?"

"You know what I want, Carrie. I'm tired of this game we've been playing. It's not fun anymore."

Her jaw slacked. The man was a moron. "This is no game, Doug. I don't like you and I'm never going to. If you don't leave me alone, I'm going to tell Mandy—*you know, your girlfriend.* Understand?"

His pasty complexion turned red, and his mouth thinned into an angry, straight line. "You're such a bitch. It's time for you to learn your place." He started toward her and Carrie's heart went crazy again.

What was she going to do? She glanced around, looking for something to swing at him. Nothing was close enough to get to.

Damn it.

Maybe if she could work her way back toward the far wall where a rake and shovel were hanging on hooks.

She took a step back, then another.

"I should have done this." He reached out and clasped her forearm, yanking her toward him. "A long time ago."

Carrie struggled to get free, screaming at him to let her go.

A knock on the garage door had them both turning. The dark-haired man from earlier towered in the archway, staring at them.

"Am I interrupting something?" He glared at Doug, who, after an intense moment, released her.

"I gotta go. We'll finish this later." Doug walked toward the door, the man standing there hesitating before

Jerri Drennen

letting him pass.

Seconds ticked by as Carrie closed her eyes. What would have happened if *he* hadn't shown up?

When she opened her eyes, she sighed. "Needed that money bad, huh?" she asked, trying to sound nonchalant, even though her whole body was shaking.

"Not here about the pants. We can discuss that later. Right now, I need help interacting with the people of this lovely town. I'm the new reporter at *The Gazette* and no one wants to talk to me. This is where you come in."

Carrie snorted. "Why would I do anything for you after the attitude I received earlier? You were rude and condescending. I don't need that in my life. As you saw, I have enough problems."

His green eyes sparkled with amusement. "Can we please start over? It wasn't really your fault the dog couldn't keep her paws off me. I am, after all, irresistible."

This time, Carrie smiled. Serious or not, his apology went a long way in her eyes, especially when he'd saved her from Doug. She clearly owed him for that, and she always paid her debts. If that meant introducing him to some people in town, so be it.

How hard could it be? He was nice on the eyes, and, maybe with him around, Doug would stay away—a more than reassuring thought to Carrie.

"Okay, I'll do it, but not right now. I have a dog to bathe. How about this evening? The Carnival's in town. Everyone will be out and about on Main Street."

He smiled, revealing stunningly white teeth. "Sounds good. Tell me what time and I'll get out of your hair."

10

"How about seven o'clock?"
"Perfect. See you then."

Chapter Two

Tate had no idea what to expect with Ms. Pruitt. He'd been completely surprised she'd said yes to his proposal, yet he wasn't going to question his luck. Not when he had someone who knew how to deal with the people of Kendall and could navigate him toward the right ones. And frankly, she looked as if she might need a chaperone after her encounter with the man in her garage. They could help each other.

He slid behind the wheel of his Jeep and started the engine. They were supposed to meet at the courthouse in the middle of town where the event was being held.

Not once had Tate been to a fair, not even as a kid. His mother had been too busy drinking herself to death to take him and his baby sister, Mya, on any family outings.

The memory caused a lump of emotion to catch like a stale piece of bread in his throat, and he swallowed repeatedly to push it down past his windpipe. He had a pen and small pad tucked into his breast pocket, ready to take notes. This wasn't about enjoying the evening. It was about finding answers to who the dead person was, and if any rumors about their death were circulating throughout the city.

Ten minutes into his drive, Tate slowed down to find a place to park, pulling up next to a white van and cutting the engine. He headed down the street, passing groups of people as he worked his way forward. The closer he got to the courthouse, the harder it became to move through the crowd. Would he even be able to find Ms. Pruitt through all these people? Hell, he didn't think Kendall was all that big. Maybe they weren't all locals and came from neighboring towns.

He scanned the area, spotting the steps to the courthouse about fifty feet away, and weaved through a family with six kids, all blonde and as cute as could be. As he glanced back at them, someone bumped into him, almost knocking him off balance. The culprit continued on his way without so much as an *excuse me*. Even Tate had manners, though they weren't taught at home. Nothing was.

He started forward again, noting how everyone seemed to ignore his presence. Not at all surprising. Small towns were cliquish, not unlike the one he'd been raised in. Hell, they'd acted as if he was invisible growing up, not once asking what was happening in the Donnelly home. Even the public school system hadn't cared that the two children in that household weren't clean half the time, never had lunch money or anything else they needed to thrive. Yet, Tate made damn sure he and Mya had survived, no thanks to his mother or anyone else from Moline, Iowa.

Tate blew out a rush of air. This town brought back all that pain—those memories he'd tamped down when he'd left so many years ago. The sooner he got back to D.C., the better off he'd be. Then, once again, he could pack that dark past into Pandora's box where it belonged.

He threaded through some teenagers, and as if the Red Sea parted, a group moved, and he spotted her—was taken aback at how different she appeared without the ball cap and windbreaker. Her hair cascaded over her shoulders in shining, auburn ringlets, surrounding a face completely void of makeup. She didn't need any. Her skin was flawless even with those cute little freckles. She wore a button-down white blouse with a pair of tight-fitting blue jeans, topped by a multi-color sweater with fringy edges, a perfect outfit for the crisp fall evening.

It was going to be harder than Tate thought to concentrate on work with her by his side.

When she saw him, she waved.

He walked toward her. The sights, sounds, and smells of food just beyond made his stomach rumble. The first thing they'd need to do was get something to eat.

"Hey," he said once he'd reached her. "I hardly recognized you without your cap."

She shrugged. "When I'm working, I want to keep my hair out of the way."

"Should we get something to eat before we get started?"

His suggestion made frown lines form on her forehead. "Okay."

"My treat since you're helping me tonight."

"Are you sure?" The woman clearly wasn't used to having anyone offer her something—a sign she was very independent. He liked that. Most of the women in D.C. were takers, expecting him to pay for everything. Carrie Pruitt was a breath of fresh air, not unlike the breeze that blew past him. And, mingling in that air was a hint of her perfume, a flowery scent he couldn't quite place. But he liked it, whatever it was—subtle, not overpowering like the women at the capital. Some days he'd gotten headaches from being near them. This light scent, he could get used to.

"You're going to have to take the lead on this adventure." He glanced around. "This is a first for me."

Her blue eyes widened. "You've never been to a county fair before?"

"Guilty as charged. So, what do these events have to offer in the form of food?"

Her eyes lit up with excitement. "Trust me. I won't steer you wrong. Come on." She took a hold of his hand and pulled him toward all the activity. Almost too much to take in.

Tate followed, even though the warmth of her touch charged up his arm—a strange jolt of energy that she clearly hadn't experienced.

The two stopped in front of a stand, where something on a stick rotated in some sort of glass case. "Can we get two corn dogs?" She looked over her shoulder at Tate, her expression priceless. "And a handful of mustard packets."

He reached into the back pocket of his jeans and grabbed his wallet, extracting a twenty-dollar bill. He handed it to the man, who gave him change.

She led them over to a table and plopped down, Tate sitting opposite her. In quick succession, she squeezed out six mustard packets into the paper container the corn dogs came in and dunked the thing into the yellow glop and handed one to him.

"You're going to love this."

Tate wasn't so sure. But he'd play along and hope he wouldn't need to spit it out. He took a small bite, his taste buds taking a moment to react. Then, he was pleasantly surprised at how good it tasted.

"See. I told you to trust me."

They both ate, Tate watching her mouth as she bit into her food. When she got mustard on her bottom lip, she licked it off with her tongue.

Jesus. He needed to focus on something other than her mouth or he was going to end up with a hard-on, and he'd have to sit at the table for the rest of the night, while somehow explaining why without looking like a *perv.* She'd never help him then.

****

Carrie couldn't stop staring at the man sitting across from her. He had the most incredible eyes she'd ever seen, intense green, yet with a sparkle of mischief to them. On his chin and jawline, he wore a day's worth of stubble, and it only managed to make him look more appealing if that were possible. His nose had a regal air, dominant to his features, yet perfectly proportionate, a small indent down the middle of the tip. To her, he was too attractive for his own good, and she'd bet her remaining bank account, he'd used his looks on numerous occasions to get what he wanted. It'd sure worked with her. Hell, his smile alone made her weak in the knees.

Carrie couldn't believe a man possibly in his early thirties had never been to a fair. It was fun to watch him take it all in.

"Okay, so what else is on the menu?" He threw his corn dog stick in the paper container and wiped his mouth off with a napkin.

Carrie glanced around, spotting the funnel cake vendor.

He watched her closely, handing her more money.

"Wow me with your next choice."

"I'll be right back." She rose, snatched up the empty

container and on the way to the vendor, tossed it into a trash can.

She had to stand in line a few minutes. While she waited, she glanced around, spotting Doug staring back at her, his eyes dark and menacing. Carrie wasn't going to allow him to ruin her night.

She ordered a large funnel cake, paid for it, then went off to the side to sprinkle powdered sugar on top, and walked back to Tate.

Carrie sat and placed the cake in front of him.

His green eyes narrowed. "What do you call this?"

"Funnel cake and it's delicious, though messy."

He broke off a piece and stuck it into his mouth, the white powder sticking to his lips.

Carrie swallowed and looked away, again, seeing Doug watching them, even though he was with Mandy. *Jesus.* Did that girl not see anything? Was she blinded by love? Apparently so since she had her arm tucked in his, looking up at him with some puppy dog expression that Carrie couldn't comprehend. Doug Walsh was no catch. Hell, he wasn't rich. Wasn't even good-looking. Mandy deserved better. What did she see in him?

"I noticed that asshole's here," Tate said, his head now turned toward Doug. "What's with you two? Or is that too personal?"

She sighed. "He can't take no for an answer. He thinks I'm playing hard to get."

"Looks like he's already caught someone. I don't get it."

Carrie glanced back at Doug. "You and me both."

"Have you talked to someone about him? That interaction in your garage today looked intense."

"I can take care of myself. You don't need to

17

worry."

"Okay." He raised a hand in defense. "I get it. Not my business. Speaking of which, do you know who lives in that house where the officer was stringing tape?"

"Vince Tripp." She grabbed a piece of the funnel cake. "I don't really know him. For a short time, a few years back, he dated a friend of mine. Their breakup was nasty."

"Nasty how?"

Carrie shrugged. "He liked to drink. A lot. She got sick of it and broke up with him. He wouldn't leave her alone for quite a while after. Wanted to get back together. Promised to quit drinking, but he never did."

"Do you think I could talk to your friend? Get some background on him?"

"I could ask her. I doubt she'd have much to say about him other than he was a drunk and a pest, not unlike Doug Walsh. This town is full of them."

"If you hate it so much here, why not leave?"

That was a question Carrie had pondered a few times. Her only answer, she had a home, a business, and a few good friends keeping her here. Other than that, Kendall didn't offer much in the line of enrichment. Then again, every town had its drawbacks.

"I own my home. I don't see a need to move. Where were you from?"

"I lived in D.C. for five years. If given the chance, I'll return."

"If you loved it so much, why did you leave?"

He shifted on the bench seat. "It wasn't by choice. I lost my job and reputation. I need to work my way back."

She frowned. "How did that happen, or is that none of my business?"

"Let's just say it was because of someone of the opposite sex. The details aren't important."

Carrie studied his face, noticing a tick in the left side of his cheek. There was a story there, but he wasn't ready to tell it, and she'd respect that.

She pointed to the confection in front of him. "What do you think of the cake?"

"I'll give it an A plus." He popped the last bit into his mouth. "Now, are you ready to go to work? I need to get to know these people. Get them to trust me, or I'll never get out of this town."

For some reason, Carrie found that last remark off-putting. She might not like everything about Kendall, but it was her home, and she needed to stand behind it, even if Doug Walsh was part of the package.

Chapter Three

On his work computer, Tate instituted an internet search of Vincent Tripp and located his social media platforms. A Facebook page and a twitter feed, though it looked as if he hadn't tweeted once in all the years he'd had his account. On Facebook he had five album files, a few posts about where he'd spent his evenings and an *it's complicated* relationship status.

Didn't Carrie say he'd broken up with her friend two years ago? Was that the relationship he was talking about or had there been a new love interest that was somehow unconventional?

Tate opened the first file and found a group of guys all holding beer bottles in several different settings. Seemed to fit what she'd said about the man—that he liked to drink.

Wait a minute. Was that Doug Walsh?

He clicked on the picture, and sure enough, it was him. Were the two friends, or just drinking buddies? He'd ask Carrie but Tate was sure the man was a sore subject with her, and he could see why. If he hadn't shown up at her garage when he had, he wasn't sure what would have happened. In his opinion, Walsh needed a punt to the ball-sack to put him out of commission for an indefinite period—deserved no less.

That was one thing Tate couldn't tolerate. Someone who didn't understand the word *no*. How many guys had he kicked to the curb who got too handsy with Mya? He'd lost count after ten. His sister was like Carrie, too pretty for her own good. Thank God his sister had met and married a D.C. attorney in a successful law firm and an all-around good guy. Something hard to come by in the beltway. Her husband could now protect her since he was so far away. He had no doubt about that.

Yet, Tate's goal had always been to return to Washington before their first child was born in January. That only gave him a few months to get his shit together and stage a comeback. Failure was not an option for him since he wanted to watch his niece grow up.

Tate knew he'd never work at *The Times* again, but there were other outlets in D.C. for a man with his experience. He'd find something.

But he'd never get there if he didn't get back to work.

He opened another photo file and there were more buddy pictures, and another set with a dark-haired woman. Not one shot with her smiling. Was this Carrie's friend? Had she already soured on the relationship when the pictures were taken? Tate seriously needed to talk to her.

"Did you find out anything yet about that dead guy off of Rueger?" Dennis Maze, his editor, asked from the doorway of his office.

"Yeah. Vince Tripp. Did you know him?"

"Barely. We didn't travel in the same circles, and I'm a decade older."

"Do you know what he did for a living? Maybe I could go talk to someone there."

"He worked over at Monroe Lumber. In the warehouse I believe—drove the forklift."

Tate wrote the information down on a sticky note, tore the slip off, and closed his browser.

"I'm going by the sheriff's office to see if he has any updates, then I'll swing by the lumber yard. If I learn anything, I'll let you know."

"Hey, before you go. I have a question. Were you out with Carrie Pruitt last night at the fair? I stopped into Lettie's for coffee this morning, and it's all the buzz."

"She was introducing me to some people. Why?"

"Because everyone knows Ms. Pruitt doesn't date. That dork, Doug Walsh has been after that poor girl since the beginning of time, and he's too thick in the head to take a hint. Warning: Walsh has a group of close friends. If he gets wind of you being seen in public with her, you might need to watch your back. He's made a point of *dissuading* guys from dating her."

"He was there last night. He saw us together. The guy was with a little blonde that Carrie said was his girlfriend. Why is he pursuing Ms. Pruitt when he already snagged a girl? That spells dog to me."

"Doug Walsh could be called a lot of things, believe me. His momma never taught him right. He's been a bad seed since high school. There were rumors he raped a girl his Senior year, but she never pressed charges. Evelyn Walsh got to her first. That woman could scare the pants off a banshee." Dennis shook his head. "The whole family think they're above the law, and not a one of them have two nickels to rub together."

Yep. Walsh's sack needs taken out. "Sounds like I wouldn't want to meet any of them in a dark alley."

"Nope. So, steer clear of Doug. He's a mean one. I'm glad Carrie had enough sense to keep him at bay. That little gal has been on her own since she moved here ten years ago, barely seventeen at the time. She worked her butt off to buy that house of hers and establish herself here in Kendall. If you could look out for her, I'd appreciate it."

"Sure." Tate was almost positive that Carrie wouldn't be happy to know people thought she was vulnerable. From what he'd learned last night, she was independent and determined that everyone crossing her path knew that. Fifteen minutes in, Tate had, and he respected her for it.

He rose from his chair. "I'll call you if I find out anything important."

Tate's first stop, Sheriff William. In the hours since his encounter with the man, he'd done some research on him. He'd been the sheriff in Kendall for over twenty years and was well respected by every business owner and council member in the city. That meant Tate needed to be on his best behavior with the man, make up for the *thanks for nothing* comment he'd made.

He was in his car when his phone chirped. He got a voicemail. Tate reached for his phone and saw it was a number he didn't recognize. He'd check it later. He had to find out if there were any new details on Vince Tripp's death.

He turned onto Main Street, spotting the one woman who'd occupied his thoughts a lot since last night—Carrie Pruitt. She was walking into the local hardware store. He'd stop and banter with her if he had time. She was fun and had a lot of spunk.

He drove past her and took the next left into the Kendall PD parking lot. He grabbed his phone and got out, tucking it into his back pocket.

Inside, he glanced around the building probably

built in the fifties yet definitely updated. Nice and clean, the floors gleaming. At the desk he was met by a blonde in a tan uniform, her hair pulled back tightly into a ponytail. She looked up from what she was working on and gave him a smile—one that was bright and friendly. "Can I help you?"

"Is the sheriff available? I'm the new reporter at the paper. I was hoping he could give me an update on the Tripp death."

Her amber eyes lit up. "You're Carrie's new friend, right? Tate, something?"

"Donnelly, and I guess, you know her?"

"She's my best friend."

"You the one who dated the dead guy?"

"Oh, no, that's Beth. She works over at Kendall Savings and Loan, and I doubt she's heartbroken over his passing."

"So, how did you hear about me and Carrie?" Had she told the woman? Was she talking about him? Did she like him?

"It's all over town. Carrie isn't going to like it one bit, believe me. She hates rumors about herself."

"She was simply helping me out last night. I'm new and she offered to show me around town—introduce me to some people. That's all, and you're welcome to spread that far and wide."

"I'll do that." She winked at him.

What was that about? Did she think he was fair game now that he'd told her the story between him and Carrie? She was cute and all, but he wasn't interested. He was here to get his floundering career above water, not socialize with the single ladies in town, unless that lady was Carrie. And that would be futile, since according to everyone he'd talked to, she didn't date *anyone*.

"Can I talk to the sheriff?"

"He's not here. He was called over to the coroner's office in Bailey. He won't be back for at least an hour."

Hmmm. What had the coroner learned that couldn't be said over the phone? This intrigued Tate and made him more determined to talk to the sheriff. Yet, he couldn't wait around. He'd drive over to the lumber yard and see what Tripp's fellow employees thought of the man and if they knew anything about his demise. Then, he'd come back and talk to the sheriff.

****

Carrie stepped into Lettie's for a cup of her favorite dark roast, her last stop before heading home. This was her one and only indulgence. Once a week. Like clockwork.

She stepped over and smiled at the teenager who was behind the counter.

"The usual?" the girl asked.

"Of course."

The teen nodded. "Coming right up."

While Carrie waited for her coffee, she glanced over her shoulder and noticed that everyone was staring at her. Did she have something on her face?

She turned away and swallowed a lump forming in her throat. The girl brought her coffee, and Carrie handed her three dollars.

"Is it true?" the girl asked, fidgeting with a paper napkin on the counter.

"Is what true?" Carrie had no idea what she was talking about.

"That you're dating the new guy in town. The one

Jerri Drennen

who works at the paper."

"What? No. I'm not dating anyone."

The girl's eyes narrowed. "But everyone was saying you were at the fair with him last night. Trudy said he's like the best-looking guy she's ever seen."

Carrie never dreamed this would happen. She should have told Tate no. Now, everyone thought they were seeing each other. "He asked me to introduce him around. He was having problems getting people to talk to him. That's all it was."

"So, I can tell Trudy he's fair game?"

"Yes, of course."

"Awesome. She'll be thrilled to hear that."

"Great. So, I'll see you next week." Carrie left the coffee shop, annoyed that the one and only time she'd been seen with a man, the whole community assumed she was dating him. This was what she hated about small-town living. Everybody knew everybody's business. Growing up, the rumors were all about her mother.

She heaved a sigh and headed for her truck. This would pass if she steered clear of Tate Donnelly.

As she was opening her door, a familiar voice stopped her. She turned and there he was, looking pleased as punch. Clearly, he hadn't heard all the talk.

"I was heading in to get a cup of coffee." He reached out, grabbed her cup and took a sip, then handed it back. "That's good. What is it?"

"Do you always take what you want?" She'd meant for her tone to sound sharp, but it came out more sarcastic than anything.

"Not usually, yet after what we shared last night, I thought it'd be okay."

26

Carrie's jaw slacked. "What we shared?"

"The funnel cake. What did you…oh, I get it." His green eyes lit with amusement. "I heard from numerous sources today that you don't date, or anything else."

"Who told you that?"

"So, you do date, then?"

Carrie wanted to roll her eyes. "No. But, who told you I don't date?"

"Where do you want me to start? First, my editor, Dennis, thought I should know when I mentioned your name. Then your best friend over at the police station said so in passing. When I stopped by the lumber yard, Frank Talbot told me to find someone more accommodating, and Manny Davis grabbed me on the way out and said that I was barking up the wrong tree, and lastly, Herman Graft over at the gas station said you were clearly into girls and that I should look elsewhere."

"You're kidding, right?"

He scratched at his stubbled chin. "I guess everyone thought I should know not to get my hopes up."

Carrie shook her head. This was humiliating. "Good to know that my sex life is the talk of the town."

He grinned. "Actually, I believe it was your lack of a sex life. I could be wrong, though."

She rolled her eyes, catching a glimpse of the window to the coffee shop where everyone inside was watching her and Tate.

"I gotta go. We have an audience."

He turned and frowned. "Before you do, what kind of coffee is that? The crap I had at Culvers diner the other day was awful. Tasted like cat piss. That stuff you're drinking, I could live with."

If he ordered the same coffee, would that make

things worse? Carrie didn't know. She should never have agreed to meet him at the fair last night. It was going to take weeks now for everyone to stop speculating. "It's dark roast. Tell the girl behind the counted that I recommended it, and if you could throw in the fact that we're not dating, I'd appreciate it."

Carrie jumped into her king cab and started the engine. The last thing she needed were rumors and innuendoes circulating about her, embarrassing since her mother had always been the topic of the day, every day. Dating this man and that one. Young or old. She wasn't picky. But Carrie wasn't her. Not even close. That's why she refused to see Doug. He was the type her mother had gone for, and Carrie needed a way to get him off her back.

Maybe Tate was the answer to that problem. They could pretend to be dating to keep Walsh away, especially now that he'd become so aggressive. She didn't even want to think about what would have happened had Tate not shown up at her garage when he did—how far Doug would have gone. She'd rather deal with rumors than the alternative. Fake dating Tate was by far a much better choice.

She'd call him later and work out the details; until then, she was going to drive home and enjoy her once-a-week freshly brewed coffee.

Chapter Four

Tate sipped his dark roast, waiting for the sheriff to see him. Carrie's friend had told him that Sheriff Williams had returned from the morgue but was on a conference call, and for him to take a seat in the waiting area. That it might be another ten minutes.

He sat back in the uncomfortable chair and took out his phone, noting two voicemails. He punched in his number and waited. "Tate, it's Carrie. Call me when you get a chance." Tate had no idea what she wanted. Yet, hearing her voice sent a little tingle down his backbone, a sense of excitement he'd never experienced before. He'd call her back once he got home.

He literally cringed at the recognition of the next voicemail. "Hey, darling. I'm calling you from my new phone. I know I told you I wouldn't bother you again, but John has been so difficult, and I just needed to hear a friendly voice. Call me when you get a chance. I miss you so much." Every muscle in Tate's body twitched. The nerve of the bitch to call him after what she'd done. He didn't give two shits if John was being difficult. She deserved everything she got and then some. He quickly deleted the voicemail and blocked the number. He never wanted to talk to her again.

"Mr. Donnelly," the blonde at the front desk said, drawing him away from his phone. "The sheriff will see you now."

Tate stood, tense as hell from *her* contacting him. "It's down the hall, last door on the right."

"Thank you."

Tate shook his head. He needed to pull himself together. This conversation with Sheriff Williams was too important to allow *her* to mess it up.

At the door, he knocked, noting the look of concern on the man's face. What did he know that was so troubling? Was it about the dead man? Or something personal?

"Come in and take a seat, Mr. Donnelly."

He smiled. "Thank you for seeing me. I have a few questions and I'll get out of your hair." Tate sat across from him, then took his tablet out of his bag and turned it on. "What can you tell me about Vince Tripp and how he died?"

The sheriff shrugged. "I can't tell you anything."

"Nothing? Does that mean it's a homicide?"

The older man rubbed at his forehead. Tate had seen his share of people trying to avoid answering a direct question. The sheriff didn't want to tell him a definitive yes or no.

"Look, Donnelly, I want to be as transparent as I can with you. Unfortunately, with this case, I just can't." The sheriff's cell phone rang on the top of his desk, and he picked it up. "Excuse me. I have to take this." He stood and left the room.

Shit. What was going on? Why all the secrecy about this guy's demise? It didn't make any sense if it wasn't murder.

He shifted on the chair, spotting a file on top of the desk with the victim's name on it.

Should he, or shouldn't he?

Tate glanced at the door, then reached for the file, opening it, finding the coroner's report on top. He read through it and his jaw slackened. The man had been missing organs. "What the ever-loving—"

He flipped to the next page in the file, which was a series of crime scene photos. He thumbed through his apps to his camera and snapped the pictures and then closed the file and shoved the thing back where it was. What he'd done was wrong, but it was the only way to get any answers. At least now he knew the man had been murdered, and he had something to work with.

The sheriff stepped back into the room, his face even grimmer than before. Knowing what Tate knew now, the man's anxiety was warranted. How many killers took body parts? *Besides Hannibal Lecter, who cooked and ate them.*

The thought turned Tate's stomach.

"Is there anything else, Mr. Donnelly?"

"I guess not. Thanks for your time."

"If I didn't say it before," the sheriff said, placing his hand out for Tate to shake, "welcome to Kendall."

"Thanks. Have a nice day."

Tate left thinking the man would have anything but a pleasant day. He had a lot to deal with. Trying to solve a murder like this while keeping it under wraps. Not an easy feat in this town. Hell, Tate had only been here a short time. Had spent one evening with a woman and it was from one end of the town to the other overnight. Keeping this a secret would take a lot of work. Tate had no intention of making it harder for the sheriff. Whatever he learned, he was going to stay mum until the sheriff found the killer and put him where he belonged—behind bars.

Right now, he'd head home. Once he got there, he'd take a look at those pictures, see if anything stood out, then he'd call Carrie back. Whatever she wanted had him intrigued. Then again, everything about her had his senses reeling and not in a bad way.

Tate turned off Main Street. Maybe he should stop and get something to eat. A Burger Barn was just ahead. He'd get something there.

He pulled into a slot close to the door and jumped out. Inside, he glanced around, instantly regretting his decision to come inside. Doug Walsh sat in the corner with two other guys who resembled him and an older woman that could likely be his mother. What was it—family reunion night? Maybe Doug still lived at home. Somehow, Tate didn't find that hard to believe.

Just get your food and get out.

He walked to the counter and ordered a burger, fries, and a drink, then paid the young lady. Tate kept his back to the group. Hopefully, he could come and go without incident.

Seconds ticked by until the gal handed him his food. He'd started for the door when Doug stepped right in front of him with his stocky body.

"Thought you could get out without saying hello."

"Why would I do that? We're not friends."

The smile he graced Tate with was less than friendly.

"Manners? Didn't your momma teach you anything?"

"Actually, no, she didn't. Now, if you'll excuse me, I've got things to do."

Instead of moving, Doug chose to lean an arm across the doorframe, the shit grin still plastered on his lips.

"Oh, really? And what's that?"

Jesus Christ. This guy was just itching for a fight. Tate had no intention of giving him the satisfaction. One brawl a year was his quota.

"I don't think that's any of your business. Now, move."

"Is this guy giving you trouble, Doug?" the older woman asked, having come up behind Tate. From the way she wore her hair cropped short, half sticking up as if she'd just gotten out of bed, and the way she dressed, she looked more like a guy.

"Eileen, let the man leave," the gal from behind the counter said, a cell phone now held in her hand. "I don't want to have to call the police again."

The older woman raised a hand. "I'm not doing anything. I just asked a question." She stared at Tate, her dark eyes shooting daggers his way, then turned that look on the woman behind the counter. He could see she barely controlled her anger. A woman with a short fuse. Doug clearly got his temper from her.

Momma Walsh. Scary like Dennis suggested.

"Then mind your own business and let the guy leave. I don't want any more trouble from you or your boys. I swear it's every time you come in now."

The woman huffed and clasped Doug's arm, pulling him away from the door.

Tate exited, feeling the heat of their glares on his back. That family had a serious problem and Tate wanted nothing to do with any of them.

****

Carrie was sitting down to eat when she heard a knock at the door. She rose and sidestepped Molly to get through to the living room to see who was there.

At the front entrance, she glanced out the window adjacent, the porch light illuminating her best friend, Emily. She quickly unlocked the door and smiled. "What you doing here? Did I forget we had plans?"

"No. I wanted to come by to talk to you about Donnelly."

"Okay. Come on in. I was about to sit down to supper. Have you eaten yet?"

"I have but we can talk while you eat."

The two retreated to the kitchen and both sat.

"Are you sure you don't want something?" Carrie asked, pointing to her plate. "Maybe something to drink. I have a bottle of wine in the fridge."

"Okay, sure. I'll have a glass if you do."

Carrie jumped up and retrieved the bottle and two glasses from the cupboard. She unscrewed the top, poured her friends then hers, and seated herself again. "So, what's this about our new newspaper man?"

"He came in today to talk to the sheriff. Vince's death, I guess. I asked about you and him. He said he'd come to you for help. That the two of you aren't dating. Is that true?"

"It is, but it isn't."

Her friend frowned, then tucked a strand of her blonde hair behind her ear. "What does that mean exactly?"

"So, I haven't talked to you for a few days. Friday, the day I met Tate for the first time, Doug came by. I was in the garage getting ready to bathe Princess. He suggested that I'd been playing a game with him all these years and he was tired of it. He'd grabbed my arm when Tate showed up. I have no idea what would have happened had he not come by."

Emily's eyes widened. "I told you to watch your back with Doug. He raped Diana Sherman in high school. Sweetest girl ever. She was intimidated by Momma Walsh to keep her mouth shut, or she'd permanently shut it for her. Eventually, she left town and hasn't come back once to see her parents. The Walshes are monsters. Every last one of them."

Carrie nodded. "I know. But I refuse to be run out of town by them or anyone else. Anyway, I had a thought on how to get Doug off my back. This is where Mr. Donnelly comes in. I talked to him just before you came. He's offered to help me—pretend to be my boyfriend to keep Doug at bay."

"I guess that means I can't ask him out?"

Her best friend sighed, which surprised Carrie, especially since Emily had always had a thing for Charlie Shillings as long as she'd known her. "Oh, were you going to do that? What about Charlie?"

Her friend's hazel eyes narrowed. "What about him? The man's either gay or a frickin' monk. I mean, you of all people know how I've spent the last five years throwing myself at him. All I've gotten for my effort was a peck on the cheek and a *thank you* for being a pal. Fuck that. I'm done trying to catch his eye. He's blind as a bat, and frankly, dumb for refusing to see how lucky he'd be to have me. Five years of pining is enough. It's time to move on. But, if you are play-dating Donnelly then I'll find another applicant. Marty Ames has a thing for me. I could go that route."

"But Marty is so…"

"I know, I know, but beggars can't be choosers."

"I think you can be a bit choosier than him, Em. He's so needy and that would drive you crazy. Give me a couple of days to think of someone else. A guy who's worthy of you. Marty isn't."

"What about you? This thing with Donnelly is all a ruse. Why aren't you looking for someone?"

Carrie shrugged. The truth was, she'd never had any offers. Tate was the first guy besides Doug to ask her to do anything. After a while, she'd just gotten used to being alone. Yet, she'd never be lonely enough to go out with Doug Walsh. He was not her type, or nice in any way. She'd seen first-hand how cruel he could be to people. How he treated the waitresses at the local café. He'd be the last man on earth she'd ever have an interest in. That's why she needed Tate—to keep him away since Doug clearly had no idea what the word *no* meant. That, and the fact he had a girlfriend, one Carrie knew personally.

"Believe it or not, Emily. Nobody has asked me out. Simple as that."

Her friend reached out and covered Carrie's hand with hers. "You know why, right?"

Carrie shook her head. "I don't. You tell me."

"Because Doug Walsh has put the fear of death in every single guy in town to steer clear of you. You haven't heard any of that?"

Carrie's jaw dropped. "Not a word."

"Wow, that man has more clout in this town than I thought."

"Why didn't you or Beth tell me?"

"We both assumed you knew and were okay with being single. I really thought once Doug started dating Mandy, you'd meet someone and do the same."

Carrie didn't know what to say. She had no idea that Doug was going behind her back to dissuade anyone from asking her out. That was absurd, yet somehow not impossible to believe now that she thought about it. How many times had she smiled at one of the local men in town and have them turn their backs on her? Now, at least she knew why. *Damn you, Doug.* He'd made her life hell for years and if it took her a lifetime, she was going to make him pay one way or another.

Chapter Five

Tate studied the crime scene photos he'd printed, annoyed that nothing stood out. Vince looked almost peaceful, sitting in a chair in his living room, his eyes closed. To anyone entering the room, it would appear as if the man had simply fallen asleep and never woke up. Too bad that wasn't the case since his organs were missing.

But why? That was the key to the murder. Who would take a heart, a liver, lungs and kidneys from a body? Then stage it to look like a natural death, knowing when the person was autopsied, that they'd find the body parts missing. It didn't make sense. Then again, not much had the past two years. The world seemed to be in total chaos, yet here in Kendall everyone appeared oblivious. Maybe it was Tate. Perhaps living in Washington, D.C. had blinded him to regular life. Maybe he was letting himself be led down a dark path where everything looked bleak, when in fact, it was just politics as usual.

Tate shook the thought. He needed to push that away for now. He had to keep focused on this murder.

Again, he looked at the first picture. Then the next.

Dammit. What was he missing?

Maybe he could do a search for bodies found with missing organs.

He quickly brought up his search engine on his

home computer and typed that in, pages upon pages popping up. He never dreamed there could be that many.

Tate needed to narrow the field. By using what, though? A list of all organs Vince had missing.

He made the change, and it indeed narrowed the field. He clicked on the first, finding it to be completely different in MO. He moved to the next, then the next. None so far seemed to fit.

Tate moved on to the next page and opened the link, taken aback at how the details were almost the same as Vince's. The victim was from Missouri as well. Bailey, Missouri, which was a few towns over from Kendall. Yet, the murder was solved. A local man in jail pending trial.

Tate grabbed a sticky note off the side of his desk and wrote down the information, including the police department working the case and the man who was incarcerated. He'd call and see if he couldn't get an appointment to meet with the sheriff about the murder and then the man in jail. The cases were too similar to not see if there was a question to this man's guilt or not. Maybe this was the work of a serial killer, and they had an innocent man in custody.

He turned off his search engine and blew out a breath, noting the time. He'd deal with this in the morning, for now he had a date to go to the movies with Carrie. This game they were playing had to start tonight. Why the rush, he wasn't sure, but she'd been determined that they be seen in public together that evening.

Perhaps she was afraid Doug would try something again and that somehow them being together would detour him. Tate wasn't so certain. A guy like Walsh didn't care one iota about right or wrong, and from what he'd observed at the Burger Barn, the family liked to terrorize whoever crossed their path. Apparently, that was Tate now since coming to Carrie's aid. He'd do it again in a heartbeat. No man had a right to put his hands on a woman who didn't want them there. Doug Walsh clearly hadn't learned that lesson, and Tate was more than happy to teach the bastard.

He rose from his chair and grabbed his car keys, heading for the door. If he didn't get a move on, he'd be late for their first date, and he was sure Carrie wouldn't be opposed to giving him hell for doing so.

In his car, he cranked up the music, the alternative rock station his jam. As he drove, he had to smile at a few of the lawns covered in tombstones and hanging skeletons, Halloween only a few weeks away.

While growing up, Halloween was the only time he and Mya ever had candy. The two would spend their evening filling a grocery bag to the top, then they'd hide them under their beds so their mother wouldn't steal any. To this day, he resented her for never having their best interest at heart.

He turned onto Carrie's road and pulled into her driveway. Before he could get out, she strode out the door and got into his Jeep.

"You're late." She clicked her seat belt into place.

"Sorry about that. I lost track of time."

"If we don't hurry, we are going to miss the start of the movie."

Tate backed out of the driveway, noting she hadn't even bothered to look at him. This was a means to an end for her, nothing more.

"What are we seeing tonight?"

"This time of the year you get horror at the theatre."

"Okay. So, I've been meaning to ask how business is for you. Do you make a living grooming animals?"

She flashed him a look that would have intimidated most people, but he had dealt with power for years. Carrie was a lamb compared to those wolves. "I own my own home. Does that answer your question?"

Tate raised a hand from the wheel. "I'm just trying to make conversation, Carrie. No need to get defensive."

"Sorry. I'm just having a hard time right now with all that is happening. Doug is cornering me on all fronts, spreading rumors that I'm bad at my job. I've lost five of my regulars, and that hurt my bottom line."

"Why is he doing that if he likes you?"

She snorted. "He doesn't *like* me. He wants what he can't have." She shifted in her seat. "You know how that goes. I think he wants me down and out, hoping that I'll come crawling to him. Using that control to force me to sleep with him. I'd never in a million years. But he doesn't know that."

Tate drove into the parking area at the cinema and cut the engine. "I had a run-in with him and his family at the Burger Barn. They seem to think rules don't apply to them."

"I guess that's my fault." She turned a sympathetic eye to him. "Doug doesn't like anyone who stands in the way of what he wants. Apparently, unbeknownst to me, he'd told all the single guys in Kendall to stay away. I only just learned that little nugget from my best friend a few hours ago. All this time, I thought it was me."

"Somehow that doesn't surprise me one bit." And it didn't. Tate had seen how Doug worked. That whole family thought they ran things in town. If Tate stayed for a while, he was going to make sure that changed—even if he had to use his voice at the paper to do it.

****

Carrie stretched out in bed and sighed. It was nice spending time with Tate as they watched the horror flick. He'd bought popcorn and sodas and seemed to enjoy being with her. But she had to remember this wasn't real. That he wasn't really dating her, just protecting her from Doug.

She pushed the covers aside and rose, heading for the shower. She had a regular coming in for grooming. A short-haired lab named Cinnamon who was a handful on a good day.

After showering, she dressed in a T-shirt, jeans and slipped into a pair of canvas sneakers, then raced down the hall to the kitchen to put on the kettle. She was headed out the back door when she heard a knock on the front entrance. "Who would be coming by this time of the morning?"

She changed directions and walked to the living room to unlock and open the door.

"Hey, Marlene." Carrie glanced at the woman's car. "Where's Cinnamon? Is she okay?"

"Yes, she's fine. I just decided to groom her myself from now on. I thought you deserved me coming by in person instead of a phone call after six years."

Carrie's stomach flipped. Why was this happening to her?

"Sorry, Carrie. Things are tight right now. I can't justify the cost."

"It's okay. I understand."

For whatever reason, she did. She just hoped it wasn't because of Doug. Carrie could appreciate if it was indeed a money issue, she had one herself, but if this was from the lies he'd been spreading, then it made her angry. Enough to spit and then have a talk with him. Make him stop trying to destroy her business.

"You have a good day." Marlene's response drew her back to her. "Again, I'm sorry."

"It's okay. You have a good day, too."

Carrie waited until she got into her car, then closed the door, tears clouding her vision. Cinnamon had been one of her regulars for years. How was she going to survive if she lost anymore?

Fact was, she couldn't. She'd lose her house, the only thing that mattered.

She swiped a tear off her cheek. She couldn't let that happen. She had to be proactive and get new business. After having her coffee, she'd go down to Main Street and hand out her business cards to whoever crossed her path. She refused to allow Doug Walsh to ruin her since that's exactly what he wanted, and she was never going to let him get his way—not ever. Even if she needed to get a part-time job to do so.

She walked to the kitchen and took the whistling kettle off the stove and poured water into her cup, stirring in the instant coffee. Carrie needed to stay calm. She could fix this if she used her head.

She picked up her mug and headed out the door. Now was the time to think long-term goals for building her business. Losing a few clients might be a good thing to make her turn in a new direction. Maybe it was time to think about what all pets needed. She'd dabbled in making her own dog treats. Perhaps it was time to implement that strategy.

She'd go to the grocery and buy a few supplies, then bake them and see if a few of the local businesses wouldn't allow her to place them for sale in their stores and maybe the two veterinarians in town. She could start out small and pray that it could pay for itself and then some. Because if this didn't pan out, she'd lose everything she'd spent the last ten years building.

As she was parking in the local grocery store, her phone chirped. She reached in her handbag and saw that it was Tate and pressed accept. "What's up?"

"I need your help with something." His voice was low as if he was trying to keep someone from hearing the conversation.

"What do you need?"

"Could you ride along with me today?"

"Where, and why?"

"The where is Bailey, Mo, and the why, I'll tell you on the way."

Carrie had plans but they could wait. Tate had helped her with Doug. She owed him for that.

"Okay. I'm at the store picking up a few things. Could we meet at my place in about forty-five minutes?"

"That'll be perfect. I have to stop at the paper and let my editor know I'm going to be gone for the day."

"Will we be?"

"Be what?"

"Gone all day?"

"That depends on what I learn. Will that be a problem?"

"No. I'm just wondering. I'll see you in about an hour."

Carrie ended the call and jumped out of her truck to go inside the store. She had to rush to get what she needed so that when they did get back, she could mix up and bake her treats. Then tomorrow morning, she'd go around to the local businesses and pray they'd let her sell them there. Otherwise, she didn't know what she was going to do.

Chapter Six

Tate pulled into a parking slot in front of the Bailey police department and cut the engine. He turned to Carrie, who looked a bit pale because of what he'd overheard that morning at the local café. Supposedly, Doug had been bragging to everyone who'd listen that he'd bagged her the night before. Untrue, since she'd been at the movies with Tate, yet people seemed to be all ears. This is what sucked about small towns the most. Truth didn't always matter when something juicy was circulating. That hadn't changed since he'd left small-town living behind.

"Don't let him get to you, Carrie. Enough people in Kendall know what kind of person Doug is. They won't believe him. Besides, a bunch of people saw us at the theatre anyway."

"I'm okay. He's such an evil minion. I can't believe he'd tell people that, especially now that he has a girlfriend. What's going to happen when she hears about the rumors?"

Tate shook his head. "The man clearly doesn't think past his nose. Did he even graduate high school?"

Carrie shrugged. "I don't know. By the time I came to Kendall, he would have already finished school."

"Maybe I should do a little background check on him and his notorious family. See what we're dealing with. That is, after I talk to the people I need to here. Can you keep yourself occupied for a while? I need to talk to Bailey's sheriff. I'll try and be quick."

"Sure. I'll look around the shops. I'll be fine."

"Okay. I'll text you when I'm done."

They got out of his Jeep and both went in opposite directions, Tate looking back at her retreating form. She certainly had a way of filling out a pair of blue jeans.

He cleared his throat, then opened the door and stepped inside the police station. A young male officer glanced at him as he neared the front desk. "Can I help you?"

"I'd like to speak with your sheriff about the Chandler murder, if I could." Tate showed him his press credentials.

The man's brow furrowed, yet he picked up the phone and talked to someone. "Take a seat, Mr. Donnelly. The sheriff will be with you in a few minutes."

Tate did as instructed, and sat against the wall and waited, thinking about all the questions he planned to ask. Tate wondered if the sheriff had heard about the Tripp murder and was speculating as to if he had the wrong person behind bars. Tate certainly would.

"Mr. Donnelly," a tall, lean-built man said, coming toward him. "You wanted to speak to me about Marvin Chandler?"

"Yes, I would. I'm curious to know if you've heard about the similarities in MO to the Vincent Tripp murder in Kendall?"

The sheriff cleared his throat. "I have, but Steven Adler confessed to the killing of Chandler. Knew some details that he couldn't have known unless he was there."

That knowledge took a little wind out of Tate's sails. Then again, he needed to know more. "Did the man know the victim?"

"They were friends at one time but had a falling out last year over a woman."

"And you think that was his motive? This woman?"

"Marvin Chandler married the lady in question and Adler wasn't invited to their wedding. Clearly, there was some bad blood between them."

"Then why the missing organs?"

"That was explained to authorities by Adler, and I can't reveal it until trial. Is there anything else, Mr. Donnelly? We have a missing person case we are working on right now. I really need to get back to that."

"How long have they been missing?" Tate asked, feeling as if this trip was a waste of time. "Less than twenty-four hours, but it's a friend of a friend. Have a nice day."

"One last thing before you go, Sheriff. Would it be all right if I talked to Adler? I'd like to confirm what you've told me."

"Knock yourself out." The man's tone had gone from cordial to irate, and Tate couldn't really blame him. He'd all but called the sheriff a liar.

"Thanks."

Tate left the precinct, thinking he'd just alienated himself from the man, but that was the nature of the game of journalism. Finding the truth didn't always mesh with authorities, especially when *that truth* could contradict their findings.

Outside, he glanced around. Bailey was no different than Kendall. All small towns looked the same. The only difference, this one was the county seat and had a jail. Tate headed for the courthouse. The prison was located directly behind the cop shop. Perfect for nailing and jailing.

The walk took him less than five minutes. The wait to see Adler would take much longer. While he waited, he'd check on Carrie.

He punched in her number, experiencing a strange tingling sensation at hearing her voice. What was it about this woman that caused him to feel excitement? It was odd.

"How's it going? I'm waiting to talk to someone and thought I'd check in."

"They have some unique shops, and I'm handing out business cards left and right. I know we live twenty miles away, but they don't have anyone who boards and grooms anywhere in town. I may get some outside business. Thanks for bringing me."

"I'm glad this trip has helped. I'll let you know when I'm finished and headed back to the Jeep."

"Sounds good. Talk to you soon."

Tate tucked his phone back into his jacket pocket. He was happy to hear that she might have drummed up some business here in Bailey. Especially since Kendall seemed to be drying up thanks to Walsh and his bad-mouthing. He still planned to do something about that when he got the chance. Doug had too much power over the people in Kendall, and he was going to put an end to that reign if it took a hit piece to do it.

****

Carrie was excited for the first time in days. She'd handed out a lot of cards, and a handful of businesses in town had offered to sell her treats if she wanted them to. The trip hadn't come at a better time, and she had Tate to thank. Ever since she'd met him things seemed to be better. Why that was, she wasn't sure, but she didn't care.

He'd helped her and that's all that mattered.

She stepped into a small coffee shop, thinking she'd splurge on a cup of French roast since things were looking up. She glanced around. The place was hipster oriented where young adults hung out, some no doubt with dogs and disposable income. She hoped they'd let her leave the last of her cards there.

She sat at a two-chair table and glanced around. The coffeehouse was unique, the far wall, half brick, the other half looking as if the bricks had fallen away, underneath painted a light golden color. There were drawings on the walls, ones that looked like they'd been created by local artists. The place was eclectic, and Carrie found it somehow relaxing. She needed that right now after hearing about Doug's distasteful rumor. The man had a lot of nerve telling people what he had—especially since it was easily disproven. Then again, she'd been surprised he hadn't said it sooner.

"What can I get you?" a young woman in a tie-dyed T-shirt and a pair of red skinny jeans asked, drawing Carrie out of her troubled thoughts.

"I'll have a cup of your French roast, and could I leave you some of my business cards?"

"Small, medium or large on the coffee and what type of business?"

"Make it a medium and I groom and board animals over in Kendall."

"Oh, cool. Sure. I'll put them up by the register. I'll go get that coffee for you."

Carrie took her phone out of her jacket pocket. She needed to watch for Tate's text.

The girl brought her coffee, and Carrie handed her a five-dollar-bill and her cards and told her to keep the change. She opened the flap on the cup top and inhaled the aromatic aroma, then took a sip, almost burning her tongue.

As she slowly drank the coffee, she studied some of the people in the room, most as she'd surmised. Young, tech-savvy, and probably still living at home with their parents.

She cringed at the thought. She'd left home at seventeen, running away from a mother who only thought about herself. How many men had she brought into Carrie's life growing up? Too many to count. And the last one was friendlier than she could handle, always touching Carrie when her mother wasn't looking. She'd refused to become a statistic. That's when she'd packed her bags, took all the money she'd earned in the part-time job, and got on a bus. She landed in Kendall and hadn't seen or heard from her mother in ten years. She didn't even know if the woman was still alive. And, she wasn't even sure she cared.

Carrie cleared her throat. Why was she dredging all this up? She hadn't thought about her in years.

Her phone buzzing had her looking to see if it was Tate. *Yep.* He was headed back to the Jeep.

Carrie rose and tucked her phone back into her jacket, picked up her cup, and left the shop. Hopefully, this would be the last time she reminisced about Anita Pruitt. It was her past and it needed to stay there.

With a lightness in her step, she made her way back to Tate's vehicle, noticing the troubled look on his face as she got inside the vehicle.

"Is everything okay?" She fastened her seat belt.

"Not really. How would you handle this situation? If you believe that someone confessed to a murder they didn't do simply out of guilt, or need of some kind, would you try to exonerate them even if they didn't want you to?"

"Why would anyone confess to a murder they didn't commit?"

Tate shook his head. "That's a good question, Carrie. I don't know, but I'm going to find out."

"Can I do anything to help? I'm free since Doug has pretty much destroyed my business until I can get some new clients."

He started the engine, turned to her, and smiled. "I'll get back to you on that. I need to go to the office and do some research first. Then I'll let you know."

Carrie sat back and enjoyed the scenery on the way home. Once they got back to her place, she'd mix up her dog treats and bake them. Then, she'd wrap them up. In the morning, she'd take them around to the shops and hope they sold while she waited to hear from some of the people in Bailey. At least she had a direction to go now and hope for a future for her business—no thanks to Doug Walsh and his bad-mouthing.

Chapter Seven

Tate couldn't get Steven Adler and the man's admission of guilt out of his head. He didn't believe him. His lack of eye contact and fidgeting in his seat said as much. So, why lie about murder? He was going to go to prison for a long time—possibly for life. Why do that to yourself if you were innocent? It didn't make sense. Though, Vincent Tripp's death didn't either. Why the missing organs? Marvin Chandler had been missing them as well. The cases were too similar not to be committed by the same person. So, why not look beyond Adler's confession? The sheriff of Bailey had to know at this point both murders were bizarre and too much alike not to be the same killer.

Where were those crime photos Tate had copied?

He leafed through the pile of papers on his home desk and found the shots from the sheriff's folder.

He looked them over once again. Nothing stood out to him. The guy looked as if he'd died in his sleep. Almost peaceful. No blood or fluids found around the body. But how did one do that with such a heinous death? Was he drugged first, then his organs removed somewhere else? That could explain the serene look on the man's face and not a drop of blood found. If only he had pictures from the Chandler killing.

Tate stared intently at the photos. The man's home was typical of a single male. Cluttered yet livable. The coffee table in front of the chair where Vince had been found held newspapers, flyers, and an array of envelopes. *Field & Stream* and *Outdoor Life* magazines were stacked in two piles on the glass top surface. A guy's guy for sure, into hunting and fishing, and drinking from the pictures on his social media pages. No different than the frat boys Tate had gone to college with at Iowa State.

He wished he could get a better look at those letters, see who they were from. Maybe if he had a magnifying glass, or software that could zoom in on the envelopes to make out the writing. Perhaps the paper had one or the other. He'd check that out in the morning. Bring the pictures with him to the office just in case. If he wasn't worried about being arrested, he'd break into the guy's home and look for himself. Though, he wouldn't rule that out if he had to.

His phone buzzed on his desk, and he picked up the phone, noting it was a text from Carrie. Simply seeing her name charged his batteries. He liked her. Then again, he'd never been good at judging women. *One* was the reason he lived here now, working at a job below his qualifications. He'd be smart to remember that—not let another woman get in the way of his success.

—Are you going to need my help?— Carrie wrote in the text.

Tate smiled. Even with all her trouble, she was still willing to aid him in his quest to find the truth. How could he not like her? She was selfless and sexier than any of those women who spent hours at salons in D.C., trying to look like supermodels. Carrie was down-to-earth real and that was more attractive to him than any debutant with fake tits and zero body fat. Not that Carrie had any that he could tell. Though, it was hard to prove with the way she dressed.

—Can we meet for coffee in the morning?— He texted back.

—Lettie's at 8?—

—See you there— Tate put his phone down and glanced back at the pictures. He had to be missing something. What was it? He knew a clue was there somewhere, but for whatever reason, he was overlooking what it could be. His gut said as much.

At that moment, Tate's stomach grumbled. Maybe that was what it was. Hunger, not instinct. When was the last time he'd eaten anything? Early that morning. Hours and hours ago. This could be why he wasn't thinking straight.

Tate eased from his chair and walked to the kitchen, opening the refrigerator, finding zero in the way of food. Three bottles of imported beer and some condiments was all that was inside, nothing for the mustard, ketchup and pickles to be put on. Clearly, he needed to go to the grocery store, especially since he'd used the last of his coffee that morning and he always wanted to have a cup or two to begin his day.

He walked back to his desk and jotted down a list of things he'd need, then went to the door where he slipped into his shoes, grabbed his keys, shrugging into his jacket on the way to his Jeep.

It took ten minutes to arrive at the nearest grocery store.

Inside, he was glad to see it looked deserted. He imagined this wasn't a peak time for people to shop. Only the pot smokers looking for munchies and the introverts trying to avoid crowds. Tate was neither.

He grabbed a cart and took off down the aisle, picking up things he needed along the way.

As he rounded a corner, he collided with one of the men who'd been with Doug Walsh the day he'd gone in to grab a burger. The angry look on his face gave Tate pause. He knew there was going to be trouble and that was the last thing he needed this evening. "Sorry," he said, hoping it would help contain the problem. "I didn't see your cart."

The heavyset guy curled his lips into a sneer. "You fucking idiot. You think you own the place, walking around like you're God's gift to the world in your fancy-ass sweater and sissy-boy slacks? I mean, look at those shoes. What are you? One of those gay boys?"

Tate glanced down at his black Ferragamos. What was he supposed to say? Not only was the man a moron, he was a bigot. More than disgusting to Tate. "Look, it was an accident, and I said I was sorry." He rolled his cart back and maneuvered around the man, only to have him slam his cart into the side of Tate's, refusing to let him pass.

"What are you, five?" Tate's anger took hold. "Take your twenty-four pack of Bud and all your unhealthy junk food and leave me the hell alone."

"Oowww, aren't you tough. I bet you wouldn't be such a smartass if I took you outside to settle this."

Tate started toward him. "You think so?"

The idiot quickly backpedaled. "Wow, wait. What are you doing?"

"I was going to help you outside. What? You don't want to go now? Were you thinking I was simply going to roll over and let you intimidate me? Oh, wait, do you even know what that word means?" Yes, Tate was going a bit far, but he couldn't help himself. The guy was a dick and needed to be put in his place.

"Is there a problem here?" a middle-aged man with an employee ID on his chest asked. "Are you at it again, Carl? How many times do I have to tell you to stop harassing the customers? Next time it happens, I'll ban you and your family from the store. Understand?"

"Hey, he ran into me with his cart, Barry. I was just minding my own business and wham."

"And I told you I was sorry," Tate shot back, sick of this whole exchange. He had better things to do with his time than argue with a mouth-breather, who clearly had a short fuse and a hygiene issue.

"Go check out now, Carl. If you aren't out of here in five minutes, you're leaving with nothing." The man was about to say something but clearly thought better of it. Instead, he turned his cart around and headed for the front of the store.

"I'm sorry about that. The Walshes are a stain on this town. Every last one of them. Can I help you find anything?"

Tate gave the man a weak smile. "Coffee?"

"Aisle four, and again, I'm sorry."

He shrugged. "It's not your fault. Have a good evening."

Tate rolled his cart toward the designated aisle, not feeling at all hungry anymore. The encounter squelched his appetite completely. Idiots like Carl made the world a bad place to live, not unlike Rita Philips and her elitist, congressional husband who, *according to her*, never had time to take care of her needs, yet sure as hell jumped at the chance to ruin his career in one fell swoop—a politician and trophy wife that Tate never wanted to see again in this lifetime or the great beyond.

****

Carrie sat down in a back booth, looking forward to seeing Tate. She wasn't going to analyze why—not today. She just planned to enjoy the feeling.

Carmen stepped out of the kitchen and noticed her. "Your usual?"

"Yes, and I'm waiting for someone."

"Anyone I know?" the waitress asked as she poured a cup of coffee and headed her way. At the table, she placed the cup down in front of Carrie and waited for her answer. "Mr. Donnelly will be joining me."

The girl's hazel eyes widened. "But I thought you two weren't dating?"

"We weren't when I told you that."

"What made you change your mind?" The girl slid into the seat opposite Carrie. "I mean, you've never dated anyone from town before. Why him?"

She shrugged. "He's nice and fun to be around. Same reasons everyone else starts dating people, right?"

The door up front jingled and Carrie looked over Carmen's shoulder to see Tate stepping into the café. He spotted her, hesitating when he saw that she was with someone.

Carrie waved him over, a strange feeling churning in the pit of her stomach. The man was too handsome for his own good. Today, dressed casually in a gray crewneck sweater and a pair of dark blue jeans. On his feet were an expensive-looking pair of alligator boots. Were they real or was he an animal activist like herself? She'd have to find out.

He arrived at her table and Carmen rose and allowed him to take the seat. "Would you like coffee?"

"I'll have what she's having?" he said, smiling at the girl.

After she'd gone, Carrie studied the man's face, noting by the deep V between his brows that he seemed troubled by something. "Is everything all right?"

"Of course. What could be wrong?"

He wasn't telling her the truth. Carrie wondered why. "So, I asked you last night in my text if you needed help with what you are working on. I never did get an answer."

"You have enough to worry about, Carrie. You don't need to add to it."

Carmen returned to the table and placed a steaming cup of coffee down. "Will you two be eating this morning?"

Tate picked up his menu. "Yes. What do you recommend?"

"The special today is two eggs, bacon and a side of biscuits and gravy. Another fifty cents and we'll throw in a fresh sliced tomato."

Carrie saw that he looked confused. "Trust me, you'll love it."

"Okay. I'll give it a go since you've never steered me wrong. What are you having?"

Carrie hadn't planned to eat until later. She couldn't afford to. "Coffee is enough for me."

"Please don't make me eat alone." His expression was almost comical. "This is my treat."

"Are you sure?"

"Yes. I hate eating by myself."

"Okay. Make that two specials, Carmen, and throw in the tomatoes."

She took a sip of her coffee and sat back against the

seat. She wished Tate would trust her enough to tell her what was bothering him. Maybe that'd be something that would come with time. Did they have that?

"I had a run-in with Carl Walsh last night at the grocery store on Main. I mean, literally ran into his cart with mine. He thought that was reason for an all-out assault. Thought we should take it outside."

Carrie's mouth dropped open. "You're kidding me?"

"I wish. I surprised him by telling him to lead the way. That's when he changed his mind. The man wasn't used to someone standing up to him. I'm thinking his brother could very well be the same. All talk and no action."

Carrie could only hope. The day in her garage didn't seem that way, but then they were interrupted by Tate. Maybe grabbing her arm was all he'd planned to do, and if that were the case, then she wouldn't need Tate to help her any longer. Perhaps that's why he was telling her this. Maybe he was tired of playing their game—didn't want to pretend to be dating her any longer since it could cut into him actually having a real relationship. Carrie couldn't blame him for that. Wasn't that what everyone wanted in life, to connect with another person? To find someone to love and be loved by?

She sighed. Would she ever find that?

"Where did you just go?" he asked, studying her intently.

"I was just thinking about what you said. I'm not sure if you're right or not about Doug. He's the oldest and the meanest of the Walshes. I can't see him backing down like Carl."

"I don't know, Carrie. I met his mother. She might

actually be the meanest of the bunch." He gave a cockeyed grin that made her giggle. She could seriously get used to having him around. If nothing else, to keep her amused. He had a great sense of humor, something lacking in most of the male population of Kendall.

Carmen arrived with their food, the aroma causing Carrie's stomach to growl. Before she dug in like a starved pig, she forced herself to wait until he took a bite, then she'd eat. The last week she'd barely had enough money to keep her lights on. That, to her, was more important than food. She couldn't keep a business running without electricity. So, this meal she was going to enjoy since it could be the only one she had that day.

"What do you think?" she asked after he'd swallowed his first mouthful.

"You did it again. It's a gift."

Carrie dug into her meal, going slowly, savoring every single bite. When she'd finished and sat back again, her phone started to ring. She didn't recognize the number but answered it anyway.

"Hello."

"Carrie Pruitt?"

"Yes. Who's this?"

"Name's Valeria Drury. I'm calling because my husband and I are going away for a few days for our anniversary and were wondering if you could board our lab, Maxwell?"

Carrie couldn't believe her luck. "Of course I can. When would you want to bring him by?"

"We're from Bailey, so it'll take us forty minutes to get there. How does noon sound?"

"It sounds perfect. I'll text you directions and I'll see you then."

Carrie ended the call and smiled at Tate. "Looks like the Bailey trip is paying off. I have a new customer."

He grinned back at her. "Good. Glad to hear it."

"Thank you for taking me with you. Hopefully, this will open a new market for me. If these people are happy then they'll tell friends, who will tell friends. Word of mouth is everything in this business."

He nodded. "I'm happy to help in any way I can, Carrie."

Carmen arrived, brought the check and picked up their empty plates, then left again.

"Thanks for breakfast."

"How about dinner tonight?" he asked, surprising her.

"I'll have a new dog. I'd hate to leave him since I don't know how he'll be without his mommy and daddy."

"Okay, so I'll bring Chinese over then? You won't have to worry. What do you say?"

"Are you sure?"

"Yes. How's seven?"

"Sounds perfect."

Tate rose, took out his wallet and threw three-dollar bills on the table, then snatched up the check. "See you tonight."

On his way to the door, he stopped at the register to pay and turned back to grin at her before he left.

The simple gesture sent her heart racing in her chest. She could get used to this handsome man's attention, and that scared her. Caring about someone had never gone well for her in the past. What if she started to have feelings for Tate and he decided that living in Kendall wasn't permanently in his plans? How would she deal with that? She didn't know. That's why it was best not to get used to having him around—just in case.

Chapter Eight

Tate scanned the photos into the machine, then brought them up on his work computer, zooming in five hundred percent. It magnified directly on the letters. He was disappointed to see most were bills. Some were impossible to view since they were covered by others.

This was a waste of time.

He panned out on the photo, noticing a mirror that caused a flash of light to stream down onto a shelf—a shelf that contained a white box with writing on the side. Tate zoomed in on it as best he could and made out a few of the letters. "F…a…m," he read, straining to make out the rest. *Wait. There was another word.* "G…e…n…e…"

"Shit. Gene. What the hell."

"Tate, I need you to drive over to Bailey and cover the Adler trial that starts today." Dennis Maze stepped over to his cubicle. "It's pretty much cut and dry but it still could take a few days. Be prepared for that." He handed him a file. "That folder has everything I have on the story. Go over it when you get a chance."

Tate quickly closed the photo on his desktop, not wanting his editor to know what he'd done. He hadn't worked with the man long enough to know how ethical he was as a reporter. He wondered what Dennis would say if he knew he'd already been to see Adler. That he'd talked to the sheriff of Bailey as well. Right now, he didn't plan to tell him. Maybe in a few days.

"All right. I'm on it." He gathered a few things, including the pictures he'd scanned and stuffed it all into his bag. If Carrie didn't have a new dog coming, he'd invite her along. Hopefully, he'd be able to get back to order food and arrive at her place on time that evening. For whatever reason, he wanted to spend time with her again.

On the drive to the county seat, he sounded out the letters on that white box. "Fame. Familiar. Family." Could be the last one.

How about Genes? That word had more letters. Genetics. That would work. Family Genetics. What the hell was that? When he got back home, he'd do a search on it. That's if he had time. If nothing else, he'd check in the morning before he had to head back to Bailey.

As he drove, he allowed his mind to wander, and he reached town and the courthouse in record time. He parked in the lot across the street, locked up and started toward the door, noticing a bunch of people standing off to the side of the building. Were they all waiting to get in? Obviously, this murder trial was a big thing here in Bailey. Then again, what else was there to do in a town this size?

Tate had to wait ten minutes to get inside and then had to empty his pockets and be scanned from head to toe. At the door to the courtroom, he showed his press credentials and was led to the area where the local reporters were seated.

He sat next to a petite blonde with coke bottle glasses. She smiled when she saw him. Tate couldn't help but return the gesture. You never knew when connections could come in handy. He didn't want to burn any bridges.

"Did I miss anything?" he asked her as he took out his tablet and brought up a Word document.

She watched him, looking somewhat confused by what he was doing. In her hand was a pad and pen. The blonde shook her head. "No, nothing yet."

"Okay. Good."

"I've never seen you before. Who are you with?"

"*Kendall Gazette*. I'm new."

Shuffling made Tate turn to see Steve Adler being brought out and seated to the left of them. Moments later, the judge stepped into the courtroom and went to sit at the front desk, peering down at them all. He was a man who looked to be in his early fifties, his dark hair graying at the temples. He had a series of laugh lines around his mouth and crinkling around the eyes. Formidable, yet friendly looking.

"What is Mr. Adler's plea?"

"Judge, my client pleads not guilty."

The whole room erupted in outrage, the looks on their faces aghast. All but Tate who was happy to see the man had come to his senses. No way did he kill Chandler.

"Your honor. I'm going to need an extension since this was a surprise to the prosecution."

The judge rubbed his chin. "All right. I'll give you twenty-four hours. We will adjourn for today and reconvene at nine tomorrow morning. I expect to be hearing opening statements then, Mr. Fleming."

The man cleared his throat. "Yes, Judge. Thank you."

"That was unexpected," the woman sitting next to him said, gathering up her things.

"Why's that?"

"Because he came forward the same day of the murder and confessed. Now, he's saying he's innocent. It doesn't make any sense?"

Little did this woman know that it did. The man wasn't guilty. He couldn't be. Not when an exact killing was committed while the man sat in jail. Obviously, he'd realized that life in prison wouldn't be pleasant, and for whatever reason, was not worth whatever led him to confess in the first place.

Tate rose from his seat, leaning down to grab his bag. He'd love to be a fly on the prosecutor's wall later that afternoon. Here, the attorney had thought coming into this today that this was an open-and-shut case. With the guy pleading guilty. Now, he was going to have to work for a conviction—difficult to say the least when the suspect was innocent. Tate couldn't wait to see what he did in the morning. He was looking forward to it. But first, he had something else to do. He needed to go home and find out what Family Genetics was and why Vincent Tripp had a box from them sitting on his shelf.

****

Carrie stepped out the back door of her house, a leashed Maxwell at her side. As she started down the sidewalk, her heart skidded to a stop. Doug Walsh stood leaning against his truck, his eyes boring into her, a cruel smile plastered on his face.

Just ignore him.

She resumed her pace, the chocolate lab prancing alongside her.

"What? No 'hello, Doug' today?"

"Fuck off. I don't need this right now."

"Oh, the language on this girl. Your mother would

be so proud."

"Actually, she would, but I couldn't care less. Now, go away. I'm working." She had to remember what Tate told her. The Walshes were all talk and no action.

She moved past him and headed down the street, the hairs on the back of her neck charged. Tate better be right about his assessment, or she could be in big trouble.

"Hey, bitch," he said behind her, too close not to have followed her.

She swirled around, tangling herself up in the dog's leash. Doug stood ten feet away, pure contempt on his face.

"I want you to tell that boyfriend of yours that he'd better watch his back. Next time he'll have to deal with all the Walsh boys."

Carrie sighed. What had she gotten Tate into? Now, he was a target of Doug's ire. She'd need to warn him right away before he found himself cornered by the despicable brothers.

"Look, Doug, Tate didn't do anything wrong." She stepped over the top of Maxwell's leash to get untangled. "This is about *me,* and you know it."

"So, what are you willing to do to protect your prince charming?" He leered at her.

Just the idea of what he suggested made her want to lose her lunch. "Not that. Ever."

He scowled again. "That's your choice, Carrie, but remember pretty boy may not look so pretty when we're done with him. Think about that." He turned around and started toward his truck.

Carrie closed her eyes and inhaled deeply. Maybe it was time to have a talk with the sheriff. Doug was getting out of control, and he needed to be reeled in. Perhaps law enforcement could make him see that there were rules he needed to follow. Though, surely, they had tried before.

She looked down at the dog and smiled. "Sorry about that, buddy. Let's go for that walk."

Fifteen minutes later, she entered her house and placed the lab into a kennel and locked the door. She needed to call Tate and tell him what happened, hope he'd watch for anything coming his way. He thought the Walshes were all bluster, but Carrie wasn't too sure about that.

She quickly rolled through her contacts and found him and pressed call. "Hey, you. I was getting ready to head over. What's your poison for Chinese cuisine?" he asked in a cheerful tone.

How happy would he be when she told him the threat she'd received from Doug? "Anything's fine but I have to tell you something."

"Okay. What's up?"

"Doug's got it out for you. He suggested if I wanted to protect you, I could do a personal favor. If you know what I mean."

"Son of a… That man needs a good beat-down. Don't worry about me, Carrie. I can take care of myself. You worry about you."

"But he threatened to bring the whole clan down on you."

"Let him try. Believe me, I can handle them. Now, back to the Chinese food. What's your preference?"

"Tate… I—"

"No," he interrupted. "You need to stop worrying and tell me what you like."

"Okay, okay. Vegetable fried rice is my favorite with some crab Rangoon."

"Then you shall have it, milady," he said with a regal air. "Now, pick us out a movie to watch, and I'll be there in forty-five minutes."

Carrie ended the call. She wished she could be as sure about the Walshes as Tate seemed to be, but she'd always been a worrier. How could she not be with the way she'd been raised? Always watching her back. Yet, Tate told her not to be concerned and right now she was going to listen—at least for tonight. She had less than an hour to shower and find something to wear. She didn't have time to worry.

It might be a fake date to him, but she still wanted to look nice.

By the time she'd dressed and chosen an action-adventure movie, there was a knock on her door. She opened it to find Tate holding a large bag, smiling from ear to ear, looking so much better than her.

Dammit. How did he always do that?

"Come on in. I thought we'd eat while watching the movie I picked. Let me go check on Maxwell, my only client's dog, and I'll bring us both a beer on the way back."

"Sounds good."

She quickly checked on the lab, who was sleeping, and then grabbed a couple of beers from her fridge and headed for the living room. Tate was taking the containers out of the bag when she returned.

"So, how was your day?" Carrie handed him a beer.

"My editor sent me over to Bailey to cover the Adler trial, which was delayed because Adler changed his plea at the last minute."

"What?" She came to sit next to him on the sofa. "I thought he was pleading guilty?"

"So did the prosecutor. That's why they asked for a continuance."

Her eyes widened in surprise. "Do you know why?"

"I imagine it's because he's innocent."

"But I heard he confessed to the murder?"

"Yes, he did, but I believe he did so for another reason."

Carrie was confused. "What reason besides guilt would a person have?"

"Believe it or not, people do confess to murders they didn't commit."

She frowned. "Why?"

"Notoriety. Feelings of guilt about something else. I'm not sure why Adler did, but when I went to see him the day we were in Bailey, I knew he was lying."

"That's why we went to Bailey? I thought you were meeting with the sheriff?"

"I did, and I met with Adler as well. That's why it took longer than I thought."

"Wow. So, when will the trial resume then?"

"In the morning. The judge was adamant about getting started."

"Will you be going?"

"Yes, so we'd better start this movie and eat so I can get to bed at a decent hour. Tomorrow is going to be a long day, and I need my beauty sleep."

Carrie nodded and went to put the movie into her DVD player. She was disappointed that she probably wouldn't see Tate tomorrow, but he had a job to do and frankly he was less likely to run into any Walsh in Bailey. Especially in the courthouse, and that eased her mind, on that front, if nothing else.

Chapter Nine

In the courtroom that morning, Tate found himself seated next to the same woman from the day before. Yet today, her smile seemed animated—why, he wasn't sure.

"Good morning." He opened his bag and took out his tablet.

She cleared her throat. "Yeah, so, yesterday I thought I recognized you from somewhere. I did a Google search." She shook her head, looking at him with distaste. "You're that fancy reporter who got caught with your dick in that congressman's wife."

Nicely put. Right to the point.

"Not exactly." He gave her a quick wink. "Her mouth was on my dick at the time. Not that it wouldn't have eventually gotten there. The woman was insatiable."

The reporter glared back. "You don't feel guilty screwing another man's wife?"

He laughed. "You think I was the first? I assure you that little piece had seen more action than half the men in the military."

Her jaw dropped. Then, with a sneer on her lips, she snatched up her handbag and slid past him to leave.

Good riddance. Hell, she'd started this. He was just playing along. Just like with the congressman's wife. She'd cornered him in an elevator on Capitol Hill. Crying about how she'd just caught her husband screwing an aide in his office. How could he say no when she'd thrown herself at him? Offered to buy him a drink. The woman wanted to get even, and he'd obliged after too many shots of Patron. Little did he know she'd become obsessed. Ruin his career with her need to see him repeatedly until they'd gotten caught. Yes, Tate could have destroyed the congressman's career as well with the secret he held. But that truth wasn't his to tell.

"Where's Candace going?" a heavyset man who'd been sitting on the other side of her asked.

"I think she got a case of the vapors."

The man frowned and was about to say something else when a door opened, and Adler was led to the table where his attorney was seated. Then Judge Briers entered the courtroom, looking like someone had kicked him in the stomach. Tate wondered what that was about.

"Mr. Fleming, are you ready with opening remarks?"

The man standing on the other side of the aisle cleared his throat. "Yes, Your Honor."

The next ten minutes were a blur of conjecture and hearsay. When Fleming was finished, Tate knew this case was over. From the start, the attorney had never planned to try Adler. He'd been hoping to call him guilty and turn out the lights on his confession alone. He hadn't been prepared for this plea, and it showed in his opening address. Tate couldn't wait to hear what Adler's lawyer had to say. It couldn't even come close to being as bad as Fleming's summation.

The man in question stood and walked over to the jury box. "I'm going to tell you about a man who was so brokenhearted over not only the loss of the love of his life but the friend he'd had since grade school, that in his grief, he confessed to a murder he didn't commit. A lifetime in prison seemed preferable to him than his other option, suicide. Since he's been behind bars, he's come to his senses. He wants you to know he's never hurt anyone. That he was the one who was betrayed by the girlfriend of four and a half years and a friend who clearly didn't think a friendship meant more than a woman. Yet, he forgave them both, only to have them not invite him to their wedding. To you, who was the better man? I think we all know the answer to that."

Tate had to give the attorney credit. He was using the sympathy card, and from the looks on the jurors' faces, it was working. The prosecutor appeared shell-shocked and knew he had an uphill battle. Tate doubted he looked forward to the climb. Especially since the defense was making the murdered victim look like a prick, and the woman who'd come between the two friends even worse—a lady sitting behind Fleming, dressed in black, who everyone now stared at as if she were vermin. She was no longer the poor, widowed wife but the lady who'd torn a lifelong friendship apart. Who, in the juror's eyes, now wore a scarlet letter on her over-inflated chest.

He'd seen this defense before, used ad nauseam to tarnish a woman's reputation. Some deserved it—some didn't. With her, he didn't care either way. The man accused of murder was innocent. Collateral damage be damned.

Tate opened his Word tab and started writing. This was still going to be an open-and-shut case, only the defendant was going to get off looking like a saint.

The man's attorney returned to his client, clearly confident he'd done his job.

"Call your first witness, Mr. Fleming," the judge said, still wearing that pained look. What was up with the man? Was he having a crisis of his own?

"We call Nancy Chandler to the stand."

Here we go. This was going to be painful to watch. She was going to take a beating. The question was, would she get through it without the waterworks kicking in? By the paleness of her face, Tate was pretty sure this wasn't going to end well for her.

As she was taking her walk of shame to the stand, Tate's phone buzzed. He glanced down and saw it was a text from his editor. He clicked to read.

—Call me when you can.—

Was it more important than hearing Mrs. Chandler's testimony?

Probably not.

Tate would stay in court until lunch, then he'd get back to Dennis. Hopefully, it wasn't an emergency. He imagined if it was, his editor would've said as much.

****

Carrie handed the leash to his owner and smiled. "Max was awesome. I loved having him."

"That's great to hear." The woman wrapped the lead around her hand. "We may need you to watch him over Thanksgiving holiday if you are available?"

"I'd love to. Just let me know which day you'll be dropping him off."

"I will, and thanks again."

Carrie walked her to the curb, then headed back in the house to get her keys, purse and the box of dog treats she'd baked and packaged. At the local mart, she'd found cute paw print stickers to place on the price tags. Presentation was everything when it came to selling a product.

She toted the box to her truck and got in, refusing to think any negative thoughts. Positive affirmations all the way since she needed this to work.

On Main Street, she parked at the hardware store and grabbed a handful of bags from the box. The owners of the hardware store had already given the go-ahead to bring in six, offering to stick them on their checkout counter. The perfect placement. It would be there for everyone to see, and she couldn't ask for anything more.

Inside the building, her lightheartedness instantly vanished. Doug and his brothers were at the front counter. Maybe she could leave without them seeing and come back later. She slowly moved a step back, then another and was about to the door when Carl spotted her and jabbed an elbow into Doug, who looked at him as he pointed to her. "Well, well, well, if it isn't little Miss Dog-Walker."

Why did he make her job sound degrading? For some reason that kicked her ire into third gear. Did he even have a job right now? If he did, he wouldn't have it for long. Since she'd lived in Kendall, he'd worked at least ten different places until he got fired for mouthing off. The man was incapable of acting like a decent human being.

Just ignore him and leave.

She went for the door, only to have him rush over to block her exit. "Get out of my way."

"What ya gonna do if I don't, little girl?"

Carrie inhaled a breath, then slowly released it. *Stay calm. Don't let him goad you.*

She clenched and then unclenched her teeth. "Please move."

"What you got there?" He snatched one of the bags from her hand and made her drop another, the bone-shaped treats inside breaking.

Carrie snapped. "You asshole. Why don't you just leave me alone?"

Doug laughed. That made her see red. She raised her hand and slapped him hard across the face, the impact echoing around the room and leaving a mark on his cheek.

Her overreaction was mortifying. She'd never let anyone rile her this much before, not even her mother's boyfriend who'd grabbed her butt on numerous occasions.

This was her cue to go. She pushed past him and ran out the door, dodging a couple of people as she raced to her truck. Inside the cab, tears filled her eyes. Why did she let him get her so angry? Now, everyone and their dog would know she'd lost her temper and smacked Doug—not that he didn't deserve a swift kick or two. But she shouldn't have been the one to do it.

A tap on her window gave her a start. She looked up to see Beth standing next to the door, deep worry lines in her forehead. She rolled down her window and wiped her eyes.

"Are you okay?"

"No. Doug Walsh needs to die."

Her friend's eyes widened. "What did he do now?"

Carrie wiped at a stray tear on her cheek. "Made me so mad that I slapped him, and you know I'm not a physical person."

Beth leaned in to rub her shoulder. "We all know how awful the man is, Carrie, especially to you. Don't let him get you down. He's everyone's worst nightmare."

"But everybody'll be talking about it. You, of all people, know how this town is."

"Let them talk. I certainly did. Follow me to Lettie's, and I'll buy you a coffee."

Carrie sighed. Maybe Beth was right. Who cared what anyone said. It was nothing but sticks and stones. Everyone in town knew how horrible the Walshes were. Surely, a slap was due to one of them by now.

"All right. I needed to drop off some of my dog treats there anyway."

"Two birds." Beth smiled and headed to her car.

Carrie was lucky she had a few close friends who cared enough to help her look past any obstacle. If she didn't have that, she didn't know how deep into a depression she'd go now.

Her friend pulled away from the curb, and Carrie followed. She could use a strong cup of coffee. Maybe it'd ease her tension. If nothing else, having it with Beth would keep her mind off her troubles for at least a few minutes. After that, she was on her own to deal with what she'd done.

Maybe she could call Tate? He had a way of making her feel better.

Wait. She glanced at the time on her phone. He was probably still in court. She couldn't always rely on him, especially since he wasn't planning to stay in town. It was best to not get too used to having him around.

She sucked in some much-needed air and took the turn into the parking area across from the café.

A jolt from behind sent her into the steering wheel. When she came to a stop, Beth was racing to her door and helped her unfasten her belt to get out. In her mouth, she tasted blood. She lifted her hand to her lips and found a gash.

That's when she looked behind her and saw him.

Doug. He'd rammed her truck with his.

He smiled then backed up and took off, squealing his tires as he drove past.

She couldn't believe he'd hit her and run.

Beth took out her phone. "That asshole isn't getting away with this."

Carrie snatched her friend's hand. "You know he's done this before, and he always gets away with it," she said, so angry she wanted to spit. "I'm going to need to take care of this myself."

"How are you going to do that?" Beth shook her head.

Carrie didn't answer. It was time someone did something about the town bully in Kendall, and it might as well be her since she seemed to be his target to torture on a semi-daily basis.

Chapter Ten

Tate pulled into Carrie's driveway, intent on not bringing up what Walsh had done to her while he was in court. His anger about the event caused his stomach to clench. Yet, he couldn't show her that, even though he wasn't happy with her for not telling him. Dennis, his editor, had. He'd been at Lettie's getting coffee at the time and just happened to step out the door. Saw the whole thing, and according to him, no police came. Which meant Carrie hadn't called them and that pissed Tate off more. Why would she let that bully get away with what he'd done?

Did everyone allow Doug Walsh to slide by—to behave badly? If so, no wonder he was who he was. Why change if there were no consequences to your actions? It was exactly like the congressman and his extra-marital affairs. With men. Aides who literally worked under him. That man was going to continue with his amoral failings as long as his wife let him. Yet, her actions had been scrutinized, and Tate was the collateral damage because of it. Not unusual in Washington, D.C. So many marriages in the governing body of the Capitol building were not what they appeared. There were secrets everywhere in the halls of Congress—some simple speculation, others circulated rumors on The Hill for years. Tate knew a lot of them, could have used one or two to keep his job at *The Times* but refused to stoop that low. It went against what he believed was right. So, he had walked away. But he'd be back. Then, they'd all better watch out because he wasn't taking another hit. Not like the last one.

Tate exited his Jeep and walked up the driveway. At the door, he took in a long, calming breath. He needed to remember that Carrie had been through enough today. He wasn't planning to make it worse. Comforting her was what he was here for, not to lecture her on what she should or shouldn't have done.

He pressed the doorbell, then stepped back and waited.

A moment later, she opened the door, and that calm exterior evaporated, his anger returning tenfold. Her beautiful coral-colored lip was split open and swollen. If Doug was here right now, he'd beat him to death.

"Are you okay?" Tate counted to ten in his head. He needed to remember why he was there.

"I'm all right." She leaned a shoulder onto the doorframe. "Do you want to come in?"

"I would." He stepped past her, then waited for her to close the door.

"How did you find out about what happened?"

"Dennis texted me. He was coming out of Lettie's when Doug hit you."

She frowned. "Half the town probably knows by now."

"I wouldn't worry about that, Carrie, but why didn't you call the police?"

She sighed. "They wouldn't have done anything. Not really. He's done shit like this before, and they let it slide. Besides, he'd just say he was getting even for the slap."

"What slap?"

"I hit him earlier and that's why he rammed my truck."

Tate fisted his hands at his side. "What did he do to make you slap him, Carrie?" *If he laid one hand on you…*

She swallowed. "He was being an ass to me at the hardware store, and I lost my temper. It was stupid, and I shouldn't have let him goad me to that point. But I did and that's why he tail-ended me."

When her eyes clouded with tears, Tate's stomach nosedived. Without thinking, he pulled her into him.

She was blaming herself for that asshole's actions. *Damn him and the mother who'd birthed him.*

Could you use the woman who'd raised you as an excuse? Not always. Tate had a shitty mother, yet he hadn't turned out so bad. In this case though, he'd met Eileen Walsh and her sons. The apples on that family tree were all rotten.

Her arms tightened around him, and Tate suddenly became aware of how perfectly her body fit into his own, the sensation overwhelming his senses. Unnerving to say the least.

A certain appendage charged to life, and his skin warmed to her touch. He huffed, trying to regain some control, only to be barraged by that intoxicating scent of hers. In all his journeys with the opposite sex, no woman ever stirred his olfactory lobe so much as Carrie Pruitt. Her scent triggered something primal inside him, but for the life of him, he couldn't figure out why.

Her body seemed to meld into his like a second skin, her nipples poking into his chest, causing his control to erode. His lips inadvertently found and nuzzled at her neck, its warmth and smell taking on a life of its own, enticing him, causing his body to burn in intensity.

He slid his mouth across her cheek, searching for and then finding hers, the flinch he received instantly making him realize his mistake. He backed away and put distance between them.

"I'm so sorry, Carrie. I didn't mean to…I better…go," he stuttered, then shook his head and took long strides toward the door. He refused to look back. He had to get out of there. His conduct was mortifying.

"Tate, don't…."

He closed the door before she could finish. He had to get away. This was far worse than being caught with a married woman. Carrie had been distraught—was bruised and hurting, and here he was trying to make a move on her. He was the lowest of the low. Despicable and undeserving of her ever talking to him again. That fact alone crushed him since he enjoyed being with her.

Outside her house, Tate squeezed his eyes closed for a second then opened them again, humiliated beyond words. He was no better than Doug Walsh. *God.* Would she think that of him? The mere idea sent his heart into his throat.

He walked to his Jeep and slid into the bucket seat, slamming the door harder than he'd intended. Maybe he was being too hard on himself. That was his hope. But until he knew for sure, he was staying away from Carrie. It was better for them both.

****

A loud noise from somewhere woke Carrie from the restless night's sleep. She rolled onto her back and glanced at the alarm clock on her nightstand. It was barely seven.

The banging started again.

She shoved the covers aside and grabbed her robe, tucking her feet into the slippers next to the bed.

She stumbled down the hall and into the living room right as the banging repeated. Who could be at her door this early?

Rubbing her eyes, she unlocked and opened the door, surprised to see the sheriff standing on her porch, a grim look on his face. Something was wrong. Was it Emily or Beth? Were they hurt? The thought gutted her. "What's wrong?"

"I'm going to need you to get dressed and come with me down to the station, Ms. Pruitt."

Why was he being so formal? Whatever was going on, it wasn't good.

"Can I ask what this is about?"

"Why don't you let me come in, and I'll wait for you to change."

"Okay." Carrie allowed him to step inside and closed the door.

She stood there for a moment, hoping he'd tell her something. He remained quiet.

"I'll be right back." She retraced her steps to the bedroom, her hands shaking as she opened the closet to get something to wear. She grabbed a pair of jeans and a white shirt off hangers and then went to her dresser to get underwear and socks.

In the bathroom, she quickly changed, then pulled her hair into a ponytail and brushed her teeth. Before heading back to the sheriff, she sat and forced her feet into a pair of sneakers. Then she unhooked the sweater off her door rack and returned to the living room.

The ride to the station was done in silence, and by the time they arrived, every nerve in her body was ready to snap.

Inside the building, the first person she saw was Emily who looked white as a sheet. Something bad had happened.

The sheriff led her away from her friend and down the hall to a back room. In all her time in Kendall, she'd never been here.

"Take a seat, Ms. Pruitt." He pointed to the chair in front of the desk. She practically dropped down, her legs feeling like rubber.

He sat across from her and inhaled, worrying Carrie even more.

"Where were you last night around eleventh-thirty?"

She stared at him in shock. "I was in bed. Why?"

"Can anyone confirm that?"

"Of course not. I live alone. You know that."

"You are dating Tate Donnelly, aren't you?"

Should she continue the lie or tell the sheriff the truth?

"We're just friends." They were, weren't they? After the kiss last night, she wasn't sure. Then again, the brush of his lips on hers clearly repulsed him since he backed up and ran for his life.

"So, no one can confirm you were at home at the time?"

The sheriff's question brought her back to the present and what could be going on here. Why would he need to know where she was at half past eleven?

"No. Why?"

"What happened with you and Doug Walsh yesterday?"

Okay. So, this was about the accident. But why would he need to know what she was doing so late at night? This didn't make any sense.

"We had a run-in at the hardware store. He wouldn't let me leave. I slapped him. He followed me to Lettie's and rear-ended me."

"Did you tell your friend Beth that he needed to die?"

Was this what this was about? That she'd threatened him in some way? Had Beth told someone, who told someone?

"Look, Sheriff, I was mad, and it just came out of my mouth. You know how that goes."

"Yes, but when the man in question is found murdered, then I have to look at it as a threat."

Carrie sucked in some air. "Are you saying Doug's dead?"

"Yes. He was found in his truck in the Marts parking lot."

How many times had she thought about this scenario? Too many to count but now that it was true, she felt numb inside. "If you're asking me if I killed Doug Walsh, then my answer is no. I didn't do it. Would never harm anyone. Surely, you know that."

"All I know is you were heard saying *he should die* and now he's dead. I have to do my job, Carrie, and to do that, I have to question you. You should also know that as we speak, two of my deputies are at your house, searching it."

"For what?"

"I've told them to be respectful of your stuff so don't fret about that."

"Are you kidding me? I don't care what happens to my stuff. I want you to believe me when I tell you I'm innocent. I was at my house all night. *Wait.* Ask my neighbor across the street. If I leave at night, the headlights of my car wake her. She's made a note of telling me that on numerous occasions."

"All right. What's her name?"

"Barbara Plano. Like I said, she lives across from me. Her bedroom window is adjacent to my driveway."

"Hang here while I call and get one of the deputies at your house to talk to her. Can I bring you back a cup of coffee?"

"Thanks. That would be appreciated."

"Cream or sugar?"

"Black is fine. Thank you."

"I'll be back in a few minutes."

Carrie couldn't believe what was happening. Her of all people. She kept to herself. Never bothered anyone and yet she was singled out because, in the heat of the moment, she said something she shouldn't have. There was any number of people that had tangled with Doug Walsh—hell, half the city hated the whole family. The sheriff needed to look elsewhere because there was no way in hell she had anything to do with the man's death.

The minutes ticked by, and her stomach started to hurt.

She glanced at the clock on the wall, surprised that she'd been there for close to two hours now. What was taking the sheriff so long?

Just then, he stepped back into the office, a steaming cup of coffee in his hand. He placed it down in front of her and sat again.

"Deputy Adams talked to your neighbor, and she reaffirmed that she would have seen you leave. I believe you, Carrie, but I must warn you that the Walshes know you were being questioned this morning. You know that family doesn't care about the law. Is there anyone you could stay with for a while? Until we find out who killed Doug?"

"She can stay with me," Emily said from the doorway.

"Okay. Great. You're free to go, and if the Walshes do anything, let me know. I'll take care of it."

Carrie rose and took the cup of coffee, heading toward her best friend. She was thankful for her and Beth. The two were truly loyal and she couldn't ask for more. She just prayed that she wasn't putting Emily at risk by staying with her. Carrie didn't know the rest of the Walsh family all that well. Had never had a run with any of them. But, if they were anything like Doug, she was afraid they'd seek her out for revenge as the sheriff suggested, and the last thing she wanted was Emily being caught in the crossfire.

Chapter Eleven

Tate entered the Bailey courthouse, work the last thing on his mind that morning. The woman he'd kissed the night before had his full attention. He hated himself for what he'd done. Carrie probably despised him too.

He walked under the metal detector, the officer standing by rushing him through. He grabbed the phone and headed down the hall. His heart wasn't in what would happen today in the Adler trial. He already knew the man would get off, especially after the widow's testimony yesterday. She, herself, said she didn't believe her ex capable of murder. According to her, she hadn't been home when the death occurred, that she'd been at her mother's at the time. Seemed convenient to Tate. Could Mrs. Chandler have had something to do with her husband's death?

Inside the courtroom, Tate opted to sit in the back instead of with the rest of the media. He didn't feel up to dealing with Candace and her recriminations—not today. His emotions were in enough turmoil.

He retrieved his tablet and turned it on as the jury and defendant entered the room.

For a few minutes, he studied the men and women in the juror's box, all different ages and ethnicities. These were Adler's peers. Some barely looked old enough to vote.

Tate had been on a jury once in Washington, D.C.,

a bank fraud case that was as close to open and shut as they came, yet two of the twelve jurors refused to give the man a decent sentence. Their excuse, he looked like a nice guy. Ted Bundy had appeared nice and cordial, an up-and-comer in the political field, and that man had turned out to be a serial killer. Appearance meant nothing.

The judge stepped into the courtroom, and Tate focused on him, the man's face looking almost green today. Yesterday, he had appeared troubled, today gaunt, with dark shadows under his eyes. Something was going on behind the scenes in that man's life, and for whatever reason, it intrigued Tate more than this trial did.

"Have you reached a verdict?" he asked the jury foreman.

His question surprised Tate. He had no idea they'd gotten to the point since he'd left early yesterday and missed the attorney's closing arguments.

"Yes, Your Honor, we have."

"So, what do you find the defendant?"

"We find him not guilty."

Tate started to type. He had to get this story written because now he was fascinated as to what was going on with Judge Briers. There was a story behind his troubled expression. He needed to find out what that was.

By the time he'd finished writing the piece for *The Gazette* and pressed send to his copy editor, everyone except the defendant and his attorney had exited the courtroom.

Adler didn't even appear happy that he'd been found innocent. Maybe Tate could get an on-the-record statement from the two before they left.

Tate walked down the narrow aisle and cleared his

throat to get the men's attention. When they turned, he reached out to shake the lawyer's hand. "I'm Tate Donnelly. I work for the paper in Kendall. I was hoping you could give me a statement and see if I could get copies of the crime scene photos that were displayed yesterday afternoon. I had to leave early and missed that portion of discovery."

The man reached down and grabbed some papers and handed them to Tate. "My client told me he met with you a few days ago. That you'd told him about the murder in Kendall that seemed eerily similar to Chandler's. That helped me convince him to plead not guilty. So, thank you. Now, they can find the real killer."

"I knew when I met him he was innocent." Tate smiled at Steve, who returned the gesture.

"I did too, but he was being stubborn and needed to realize that his life was still worth living. Anyway, I have to get across town." He glanced at his watch. "I'm already ten minutes late. It was nice meeting you, Mr. Donnelly."

"You as well."

Tate followed both men out of the courthouse and left them to head for his car, noting another man walking out the side exit. Was that the judge? It sure looked like him.

He watched as the man got into a dark blue SUV. Maybe he could follow him and see where he ended up. There was something strange going on with the man. His gut was telling him to find out what.

He pulled out of the visitor parking lot and eased in behind the judge, keeping a safe distance. No way did he want to get caught tailing a county official. He could get thrown into jail for stalking.

The judge made a left turn, then a right onto the main highway going the opposite direction from Kendall. A mile out, he turned into a hospital and parked his vehicle in designated parking.

Did he have an ill family member? Could that be why he'd appeared distracted?

Tate parked and got out. He'd gone this far. He might as well see who the judge came to visit.

Inside the double doors, he caught a glimpse of the judge stepping onto the elevator, the car dinging on the third floor.

Tate took the stairs and was lucky to see the man walking down the long hallway to the end. He glanced around for a few seconds, nothing indicating what floor they were on. Was it Geriatrics? Obstetrics? Pediatrics? Surgical, maybe?

He strode down the hall, walking past a nurse who smiled at him before entering a room.

At the end of the hall, Tate stopped. Just beyond him was a glassed-off area. Why would the judge be here? Inside, a partition made it impossible to see anything. That was as far as he was going since the sign said Authorized Personnel Only.

"Can I help you," the nurse from before asked.

"I think I'm lost. I'm looking for Geriatrics."

"Geriatrics is on the second floor. This is critical care."

"Okay. Thank you."

Tate retraced his steps back to the elevator and returned to the ground floor. This was a crazy idea yet he had learned something. The judge had someone he cared about in an isolated area on the critical care floor of the hospital. Now, Tate needed to find out who and why they were there. Hopefully, an internet search could reveal something that would give him an answer.

****

Carrie stuffed some clothes into her overnight bag, then went to the bathroom to get her toiletries. She tucked all she'd need into a smaller bag, then walked back into her bedroom. She looked around, knowing she'd probably forgotten something.

The last time she'd had to do this, she'd left her hometown and got on a bus traveling south. That's how she'd ended up in Kendall. Was she going to have to do that again?

She shook off the thought and returned to Emily, who was waiting for her in the living room. She'd wanted to come alone, but her friend refused to let her. Maybe she knew the rest of the Walsh clan better than Carrie did.

"I think I have everything."

"If you don't, you can borrow something from me." Emily smiled.

"I think this whole thing is crazy. I don't know why I can't stay here. I didn't do anything wrong."

"I get your frustration, Carrie, but it's safer for you right now."

Carrie sighed. "I guess you're right. I don't have to be happy about it though, do I?"

"Of course not. Now, go lock up and make sure everything's turned off. You want a house to come back to when you can."

"Okay. I'll only be a minute." Carrie checked the back door and turned a light on in the kitchen. She didn't want to come home to find all her belongings stolen.

On returning, she found Emily at the front door

waiting for her. She leashed Molly and they stepped out of the house. Carrie locked up, then walked to Emily's car. She was leaving her truck here to make it look like she was home. She wouldn't need it anyway since Emily lived close to Main Street, and she could walk if she needed anything. Not that she had much money for that. She was broke.

"Let's get some lunch at Lettie's. It's on me."

"Do we have to? I'm sure everyone has heard about my trip to the police station by now. They'll all stare at me. Wondering if I'm a killer."

"If they say anything, you can set them straight. You know you can't hide out. It'll make you look guilty."

"We'll have to drop off Molly first."

Carrie wasn't sure if this was the right way to handle this mess. The Walshes weren't real popular in Kendall, but Doug did have a handful of friends that could cause problems if they wanted to. Hopefully, none would be in Lettie's.

Emily drove to her house, and they placed the dog and bowls in the kitchen, then returned to the car and headed for the café. They found a spot across the street.

Carrie inhaled a cleansing breath and opened the car door. She would act like nothing had happened and hope everyone else did too.

Inside the restaurant, they found a booth and sat down across from one another.

Carmen brought them both water and silverware. "Do you two know what you're going to have?" She took a pad and pencil from the pocket of her apron.

"Is there a special?" Emily asked.

"Yes, we have Lettie's famous meatloaf today with mashed potatoes, gravy, and buttered corn."

"What do you think?" Emily asked Carrie.

"That's fine with me."

"Give us two of the specials and some sweet tea."

"Okay. I'll be right back."

Carrie leaned into her seat, feeling drained from the day's events. She needed to put it all behind her, but it was going to be hard. How many people were brought in on suspected murder? Probably only her today. It was mind-boggling to think that Doug was dead.

Who could have done something like that in Kendall?

Inadvertently, Tate popped into her head. He'd had a run-in with the Walshes. Could he be capable of such a thing?

No. Tate was a good man. Wasn't he? He'd looked angry when he saw her injury and knew Doug had inflicted it. Would he be mad enough to find him and kill him?

"What is running through that mind of yours?" Emily reached across the table and squeezed her hand.

Carrie frowned. Her friend knew her too well. "Nothing really."

"Hah. You forget how long we've been friends. Now, tell me what you were thinking about."

"I was thinking about Tate Donnelly and how mad he was last night when he saw my lip."

"Are you suggesting that he could have killed Doug?"

"Of course not. That's stupid. Who am I to him anyway? Nobody."

"So, why was he angry then?" Emily asked, her gaze intent on Carrie's.

She suddenly felt uncomfortable. Carrie hadn't told

anyone about the kiss, or his reaction to it. She wasn't sure what had even happened. He'd held her, made her feel things no man had made her feel before. Then, when his mouth met hers, the pressure had made her flinch and caused him to bolt out the door. Left her standing there feeling like a fool?

Wait. Oh my God. She hadn't meant to recoil, but the force of his mouth on her swollen lip had caused her to react. Had Tate thought she was repulsed by his kiss?

"Here you go." Carmen placed two steaming plates down on the table then ran back for their glasses of iced tea. "Enjoy."

Carrie stared at the food, playing last night's events over and over in her head. The more she relived it, the more she realized this was all a misunderstanding on both of their parts. She needed to talk to Tate, tell him the truth and go from there.

That settled, she picked up her fork and scooped up a bite of meatloaf, popping it in her mouth, the flavor overwhelming her taste buds. As she was taking her second bite, the café door jingled, and she glanced up to see Hank Graves stepping inside. Carrie knew he was a friend of Doug's. She prayed he wasn't going to make a scene. That was the last thing she needed.

She ducked her head, hoping he wouldn't notice her.

"Is my pickup ready, Carmen?" he asked.

"Let me go check."

Carrie snuck a peek at the front and saw Hank standing next to the cash register, digging money out of his wallet. *Just keep him occupied. Don't let him see me.*

"You okay?" Emily's question drew her attention back to her friend.

She tried to whisper for Emily to keep it down, but

it was too late. Hank turned and saw Carrie, his eyes narrowing.

"Shit," she said as he headed toward them.

"You got some nerve showing your face in here," he said, practically fuming.

Emily put her fork down and rose, coming face to face with the man.

"Carrie didn't do anything. Don't believe me, go ask the sheriff."

"Look, Emily," he said, pointing his trigger finger at her. "I have no beef with you. Doug was my best friend. So, please stay out of this."

"Well, Hank Graves, Carrie's my best friend, and she had an alibi for last night. Go interrogate someone else."

He looked at Carrie, who nodded.

"Hank, your food's ready." Carmen held up a large bag. Talk about perfect timing. Carrie would have to thank her later.

Emily refused to stand down as Hank contemplated what to do. "You have a loyal friend, Carrie. You're lucky." He then winked at Emily and stalked to the front.

Emily looked at Carrie, then slid back into the booth and grinned. "What was that wink about?"

"Surely you know Hank's had a thing for you since I've known you," Carrie said, surprised that her friend had to ask.

Emily's eyes widened. "No way."

"Yes, way. Oh my God, you didn't know?"

"No. I've been too hung up on Charlie to notice anyone else. Too bad the man has no taste in friends. That's a deal breaker."

"Why is that?" Carrie asked. "He's had the hots for

you. Can't be all that bad."

"True, but who could be best friends with Doug Walsh? I just couldn't date a guy who's that stupid."

Carrie burst out laughing. Leave it to her best friend to lighten the mood after the day she'd had.

"Let's finish eating and then go by the Liquor Locker and pick up a bottle of wine that we can enjoy while watching *The Bachelor* on TV tonight."

"Do you seriously watch that crazy show?"

Her best friend gave her a goofy grin. "I do, and by the end of the night, you'll be watching it, too."

Chapter Twelve

Tate drove past Carrie's home, his heart rate picking up speed when he saw her truck parked in the driveway. Too bad he couldn't stop. Not after what had happened between them.

He passed, unsure of what to do with the rest of his day. Maybe he'd get a six-pack and some fast food, then go home and do an internet search on Judge Brier—find out who was in the hospital where the man visited.

He turned left onto Main and drove past Lettie's. The town's only liquor store was two blocks down.

Tate parked his Jeep in front of the brick building next to a red SUV and got out. As he headed for the door, he saw Carrie's friend Emily from the police station step outside, laughing. Another woman stood behind her.

His step faltered, and his heart started on that uphill climb again.

Carrie.

She saw him and froze.

"Hello," Emily said after a few moments of silence.

What was he going to say? "What brings you ladies here?"

Emily lifted a bottle in her hand. "Came to get some wine. How about yourself?"

"Picking up a six-pack before heading home."

Carrie's friend smiled. "We don't want to keep you. We have a date with a bachelor."

His attention flew back to Carrie. Who could the man be?

"You have a date?" he asked her.

"God, no." Carrie looked at Emily, who'd started laughing again.

"It's a reality show. We're going to my place to watch it."

Emily's answer relieved his mind. Later, he'd analyze why. "Oh, okay, I see. Have a nice evening."

"Before you go, Tate. Could I have a few minutes of your time?" Carrie asked, signaling for her friend to go ahead to the car.

"Sure." It was hard to even face her after what he'd done.

"So, I wanted to talk about last night. I think you misunderstood my reaction to your kiss."

Tate swallowed hard. "How so?"

"I want you to know that it wasn't your kiss that made me flinch. It was my swollen lip. The pressure hurt a bit."

He let out a deep sigh. "Of course, it did." What the hell was he thinking? So, instead of being disgusted by him, he'd caused her pain. Which was worse? He wasn't sure.

"I'm sorry, Carrie. I don't know what the hell came over me."

"It's okay, Tate. Really."

He cleared his throat. "Okay. Enjoy your evening."

"Did you hear about Doug?"

Tate's anger flared. "What did he do now?"

Her eyes widened. "He's dead. Someone killed him last night."

"What? Why didn't I hear about this?" *Remember*

you were out of town all day.

"The sheriff had me in for questioning this morning. I was lucky to have a nosy neighbor who could tell him I was home when Doug was killed. Otherwise, I'd still be there."

"Why in the hell would he think you'd have anything to do with his death?"

"Because of what happened yesterday between us."

"Wow. I thought living in this town would be dull on a good day and here we've had two murders in as many weeks."

"What? Are you saying that Vince's death was suspect? I thought he drank himself to death or had a heart attack."

Shit. Tate probably shouldn't have revealed that fact to Carrie. "No one is supposed to know. I might have seen something on the sheriff's desk I shouldn't have. But please don't tell anyone about this. The man could run me out of town."

She studied him intently, almost uncomfortably so. "Is this why you went to Bailey to meet with their sheriff before that man's trial started? Are these murders somehow related?"

"I'm not sure yet. There are some similarities in the cases."

Her eyes widened again. "Is this a story you're working on then?"

"Maybe, but like I said, please don't say anything to anyone."

"Let me help you, Tate. I have nothing to do right now, and I'm stuck staying at Emily's because the sheriff's concerned for my safety."

"What? Why?"

"Because everyone in town knows the sheriff questioned me. I'm sure Eileen Walsh and Doug's brothers have heard that as well. You know how they are? They don't care about the truth. They'll want to see someone pay for his death."

Tate didn't like this. The Walshes were dangerous and Carrie staying at Emily's didn't make him feel any better. Two vulnerable women alone, with them on the warpath.

"Where was Doug found?" *And did he have all his organs intact?*

"In the mart's parking lot," she said, looking over at the SUV where Emily sat, then returning her attention to him.

"Did the sheriff say how he was killed?"

She shook her head. "No. I couldn't believe he'd think I was capable of something so horrible. Do you think the person who killed Vince and the man in Bailey could have killed Doug? How do we find out?"

"Whoa, Carrie." He put his hands up in a defensive gesture. "We are not going to find out. It's too dangerous for you to get involved."

"I'm already involved since the Walshes probably think I did it. You need to let me help find his killer so I can clear my name to them and anyone else in town who might think I'm guilty."

Tate never felt so frustrated. He understood her desire to do that, yet he thought it was too risky to include her in his investigation. If nothing else, because he'd be forced to spend time with her and that would be harder on him than on her. Even now, he'd give anything to pull her into his arms and kiss her senseless.

Time to get out of here.

"Look, Carrie, I can't do this right now. Can we talk about it tomorrow?" Her defeated look sent his heart into his throat. "All right. You can help. I'll pick you up in the morning. We can get started then."

She smiled, which had his heart pumping crazily in his chest. *Rinse. Repeat. Damn.* The woman clearly had power over his emotions, and he barely knew her. What was going to happen when they spent hours working together in close quarters? Life was going to be pure hell for him.

****

Carrie jumped into her friend's SUV and snapped the seat belt in place. She couldn't wait to help Tate find the truth. Growing up, she'd read all kinds of sleuthing stories, escaping real life. Books had helped her cope with her mother's turbulent ups and downs. Tomorrow was going to be fun for her, especially when she'd be with Tate. There wasn't once in his presence that she didn't feel safe, something she had never really experienced with a man before. The guys her mother brought around, and Doug, had always kept her on guard, but Tate was different. She was thankful for that.

Emily pulled into her driveway, and Carrie unclicked her seat belt and was about to get out when a truck squealed to a stop behind them. "Crap," Emily said, then looked at Carrie. "It's Eileen Walsh. Stay in the vehicle. I'll take care of this."

Her friend exited and walked toward the back as the woman was headed up the drive. "I want to talk to her," Eileen said, her voice loud and raspy.

"Carrie's been cleared of Doug's murder, Eileen. Now, get back in your truck and go home."

"Right." The woman huffed. "Like you'd tell me the

truth. She and Doug argued at the hardware store yesterday, and she was heard saying that he needed to die. She killed him and she needs to pay."

"No, she didn't. Talk to the sheriff. She has an alibi for when Doug died. Go ask him."

"I'll get her. You wait and see."

"I get that you're upset, and I'll let that threat slide for now, Eileen, but you'd better hope nothing happens to Carrie because you'll be the first to be implicated."

"Like I give a shit. My baby's dead."

"I know, and I'm truly sorry for your loss, but as I said, Carrie didn't do it. Let the sheriff find out who did."

The woman stared into the back glass of the SUV, and Carrie almost turned away. The older woman didn't believe Emily, and that spelled trouble.

Eileen whirled around and got back into the truck and took off, speeding down the road.

Carrie exited the SUV and came around. "I shouldn't be here. I'm putting your life at risk."

"Nonsense. I can take care of you and myself. I'm a cop, remember?"

"I know but I feel bad."

"Don't. Now, let's go and enjoy our evening. To hell with Eileen Walsh and all her backwoods bullshit. I swear that whole family stepped off the screen of *Deliverance*."

Carrie couldn't help but smile at her friend's reference. She was right. The Walsh family did seem the type to make people squeal. Disturbing to say the least and disgusting to boot.

"Come on. Stop worrying. One glass of wine and you'll forget all about her."

"I hope you're right."

Carrie walked to the back of the vehicle and popped the hatch, grabbed her bag, then followed her friend into the house. She was going to try to put everything aside, at least for the night. She could reexamine it all tomorrow when she was with Tate. Maybe something there could help them figure out who could've wanted Doug dead—besides everyone who ever had a run-in with the bully. Was there even a single member of Kendall who hadn't been pushed around by the guy?

No one she could think of.

Carrie toted the bag down the hall and plopped it down at the end of the guest room bed. She'd spent the night at Emily's before and knew her way around the house.

Before she could leave the room, her best friend entered, holding two glasses of red wine.

"Come on. I'll catch you up on what you've missed on *The Bachelor* before it starts."

Carrie had to force herself not to roll her eyes, then took the glass from her friend and walked to the living room. She took a seat on the sofa, sucking down a large gulp of the Cabernet.

Glass shattering had her and Emily running toward the noise. In the kitchen, the two found a brick on the floor along with glass from the window it came through.

"Oh my God." Carrie knew full well who had done the deed. "I've been here less than ten minutes and you have a mess. I can't stay here. I'm putting your life in jeopardy."

"Come on, Carrie. This isn't your fault. I'll call the station. See if I can't get a patrol car to come by and watch for trouble. I'm not in the least worried."

Her friend didn't look concerned, but that wasn't the

point. She now had a broken window because of Carrie. What else could happen before Doug's murder was solved? Too many things to even imagine. She couldn't do this to her best friend.

"I gotta get out of here. I'd never forgive myself if anything happened to you, Emily."

Her best friend came over and shook her shoulders. "You're being ridiculous, Carrie. No one wants to hurt me. They're after you. You aren't leaving. End of story. Now, help me clean this glass up, and I'll get some cardboard to cover the window until I can get it fixed."

Carrie had never seen her friend so stern with her. This was the woman the public dealt with, the officer who Carrie hadn't seen before today. Maybe she could hold her own and protect her from anyone.

"Okay," she said, walking to the closet next to the pantry to get her broom and dustpan. Carrie had to remember that her best friend coped with sex discrimination every day on the job, Emily didn't need that same crap from her—the one person who should always have her back.

Chapter Thirteen

Tate parked in front of Emily's home and cut the engine. That morning, he'd stopped by the paper and finished up the brief piece on Walsh's death, then left again.

He'd spoken to Dennis the evening before, who'd suggested he go by the police station to see if there was a press release on anything evidentiary about Doug's murder. Nothing was available, and the sheriff had already left for the day, so he couldn't talk to him. Today, hopefully, they'd be able to give him something substantial because the story he'd written was nothing more than an obit on the man. He needed a follow-up, and he hoped the sheriff could give him at least cause of death.

The clink of the front door to the house drew Tate back to the present. He was instantly mesmerized by Carrie as she walked toward him. She was dressed in something he'd never seen her wear before—a white, gauzy blouse and a pair of black slacks that hugged her slim hips. The woman could tempt a saint, and Tate was far from that.

Pull your tongue back in your mouth.

She opened the passenger door, got in and fastened her seat belt, then turned to him and smiled. "Thanks for letting me come with you today. I needed a distraction. So, where do we start?"

Tate cleared his throat and forced his libido down. "I need to run by the police station and find out if they have any updates on Doug's death. Then we'll go talk to the mart's employees. Maybe someone working that night saw something that could help find his killer."

She nodded and shifted on the leather seat. Was she as nervous as he was? Since their kiss, he felt like an adolescent teenager around her.

Tate glanced over his shoulder and pulled away from the curb, on his way to Main Street. "So, Carrie, tell me something I don't know about you.

"Like what?"

"Oh, I don't know. Let's start with childhood. Your mother. Was she more like June Cleaver or Peg Bundy?"

Her brows drew together.

"Was that too personal a question?"

"No, it's just that she wasn't really like either," she said, then glanced down to her lap.

Looked like he'd once again stuck his foot in it. He seemed to be good at that with her.

"I take it your mom's a sore subject?"

She shrugged. "Kind of. She wasn't around much, and when she was, she always had a male companion tagging along."

"Wow. That's weird. Sounds like we had the same mother."

She looked up at him. "Really?"

"Yeah, mine was a real piece of work. Me and my baby sister were lucky we had each other. We pretty much raised ourselves."

"Are you two still close?"

Tate smiled. "Yep. She moved to D.C. to be near me. That's where she met her husband. They're expecting a baby in a few months. I'm going to be an uncle, and here I am miles away."

"Want to talk about that? How'd you end up in Kendall?"

"I needed a job and Dennis offered me one." It was a partial truth. He wasn't ready to tell her the rest. Not yet. Because it didn't look good for him out of context. Hell, it didn't look great either way. Right now, he didn't want her thinking poorly of him.

She nodded. "Having a sister or brother might have been nice. But then again, I wouldn't have wanted to subject them to what I went through. My mother wasn't at all choosy about the men she brought home."

That information was tinged with undertone, and Tate could only imagine why. As a vulnerable girl, being in the hands of degenerates, elicited all sorts of negative connotations. All made him want to lose the cup of coffee he'd had earlier at the paper. Tate had always been there to protect his sister, Mya, from grabby hands. Carrie hadn't had that.

He cut right and maneuvered into a parking slot in front of the station. "You wait here. This should only take a few minutes."

Tate stepped into the building, work the last thing on his mind. Thinking about Carrie and what might have happened to her charged his adrenaline. Then again, Ms. Pruitt seemed tough. He was sure she didn't sit back and take any kind of abuse.

At the front desk, Emily sat. When she saw him, she smiled. "Good morning, Mr. Donnelly. What can I do for you today?"

"I came in to find out if there were any updates on Doug Walsh's murder?"

She grabbed a sheet of paper from a stack off to the side and handed it to him. "That's everything that the press is allowed to know about the case."

"Okay, thanks. You have a great day." Tate glanced at the release on the way out. The man was shot. That didn't fit the other men's MO. So, the deaths were probably not related. Not all that surprising. Walsh probably had a lot of enemies who wanted him dead.

Outside, he took a breath and walked to his car. Carrie was on her phone talking to someone.

As he opened the door, he caught the tail end of her conversation. It clearly wasn't someone she wanted to speak to.

"Don't call me again," she said, tossing her phone in her handbag.

"Do I want to know who that was?"

She shook her head. "It was nobody important."

"You know, if the Walshes are harassing you, you can tell the sheriff. He could put a stop to it."

"No. Doing that would only escalate the problem. Let me handle this, Tate."

He clutched the steering wheel, then started his Jeep. "How about we have breakfast and go over the crime scene photos from both murders before talking to people at the mart? I studied all of them until I went blind. Maybe you can see something I can't." Right now, Tate needed to concentrate on the two murders with missing organs.

"Okay, but you are going to have to buy breakfast because I'm flat broke."

"You're helping me with work, Carrie. Consider it payment for that."

She stared intently at him. He wasn't kidding but she

thought he was. Hell, an extra pair of eyes went a long way in this business. Buying her breakfast was the least he could do.

In less than five minutes, they were inside the café and seated in the back booth. The place was empty since it was after ten. This gave them the privacy they'd need to go over the photos.

The waitress took their order and poured them coffee. When she'd gone, Tate handed Carrie the file of pictures from the crime scene, placing his hand on top. "Are you sure you want to see these? They're not fun to look at."

"Yes. I'm sure."

He removed his hand and took a sip of his coffee, his eyes focused on her features. Her eyes widened but she continued to leaf through the pictures, one at a time, hesitating over a photo, then another.

The food arrived and she quickly closed the folder while the waitress served them.

When she'd left again, she reopened the file and took out two pictures. "So, you circled this box in the background on this shot from Vincent's murder scene, right?"

"Yes. I was going to do some research on that company. I'd never heard of them before."

"Did you notice on the coffee table from the case in Bailey, there was also a white box? You can't make out the name on it but it's the same size and shape."

"What?"

Tate took both photos and examined them again. Carrie was right. There was a box on top of the table, covered with letters.

"I've stared at these photos for almost two days and

hadn't seen this. You definitely earned your breakfast, and frankly lunch and dinner today."

She smiled, looking pleased with herself. She needed to be. He might not have ever made the connection. So, two dead people possibly had genetic testing kits and were missing body parts.

If Tate had to wager a bet, someone had murdered these men for their organs and used the kit to find the genetic match. Was it done randomly though, or was there more to it than that? That's what he needed to find out and in a hurry before more people were caught in this heinous web of possible organ harvesting.

****

Carrie was happy that she could help Tate with finding something in the crime photos. She never thought she'd ever see such things in her lifetime. He had a fascinating job, if not a bit morbid. Though, Vincent looked like he was asleep. The only difference was that he was pale as a ghost.

She quickly finished her breakfast and shoved the plate to the end of the table. "Now, we go to the mart and talk to people?"

"Do you know anyone who works there?" he asked, then gulped down the last of his coffee.

"Debbie Manning, who I dog-sit on occasion for does. She's a cashier."

He took out his wallet and placed a twenty on the table. "Does she work every day?"

"That I couldn't tell you. But if I see her, I'll point her out to you."

The waitress returned to their booth. "Can I get you guys anything else?"

He looked at her to reply.

"Nope. I'm good."

He handed her the money, then rose. They met the waitress at the cash register for his change. He quickly handed her a tip and they left the café.

On the way to the mart, Carrie remained quiet. Suddenly being with him warmed the air around her. He was so handsome and self-assured yet not at all cocky. She really liked that about Tate.

"Is everything okay?" he asked when they were halfway to the store.

She glanced at him and smiled. "Everything's fine. I'm just enjoying the ride."

"All right. So, we talked about your mom, but what about your dad? Was he around?"

Carrie shook her head. "She told me he took off as soon as he learned of my existence. All I have is a name."

"You never tried to find him?"

"Why bother? He clearly wasn't interested in being a part of my life. What about yours?"

"Mine died right after Mya was born. A car accident. I think his passing sent my mother off the deep end. She drank every day after until she died a few years ago."

Carrie reached out to touch his arm. "I'm sorry."

He shrugged. "Like I said, we raised ourselves. I really couldn't call her a mother."

They pulled into the parking lot of the mart and parked. "We'll just go in and see what we can learn."

The two entered the department store. Carrie glanced around, looking for Debbie at the front where the checkouts were.

"You see her?" he asked, so close she hadn't realized he'd moved. His lips were practically on her neck and the hair there bristled.

She sucked in some air and took a step forward, needing distance. The man had a strange affect on her body, and she didn't know what to make of it. "While we are here, I might as well pick up a few things. You want to grab a cart?"

"Sure. I'll be right back," she said and took off to find one. A few minutes away from him hopefully would help center her—get her mind back on safer things.

As she stepped out to the front, she came to a screeching halt. Doug's brother was standing behind a cart, glaring at her.

She swallowed hard, wanting to escape but knowing she had to stand her ground. Carrie didn't do anything, and she wasn't going to cower like she had.

"You have a lot of nerve showing your face around town. With that reporter no less."

She retrieved a cart and started back inside, Carl blocking her path. "Get out of my way or I'll call security."

"No need for that," Tate said as he came and stood next to her. "Do you always harass people at stores? Get the hell out of here before I take a swing at you."

The two men stared at one another for a few seconds and then Carl pushed the cart away and left, almost tripping over his feet on the way out.

"Don't let that family intimidate you, Carrie. They're just seeing how far they can push."

"I know. He refused to let me get by."

He winked at her. "Next time just run him over with the cart."

Carrie couldn't help but laugh. Tate had a way to lighten a mood no matter how dire the circumstances.

"So, what do we need to find while we look for

Debbie?"

"I have a list." He reached into his jacket pocket and pulled out a piece of white paper and opened it up.

"First on the list, shampoo."

"That, I believe, is in aisle six."

She pushed the cart ahead and started down the narrow walkway, glancing over her shoulder to see if Tate was following. He was, but his focus seemed to be on her backside. He clearly had eyes for her, too. Maybe that wasn't a bad thing. She was single. He was single. Why not enjoy what he could offer her? When was the last time she'd had sex with a man?

She gulped. Had it been that long? Jeez, what was wrong with her? Building her business had kept her focused, and no one but Doug had ever asked her out. Hell, it was time to get back in the swing of things and hope it was better than the last time. Another reason for her dry spell.

She smiled. Tate was in big trouble, and he didn't even know it yet. "So, what kind of shampoo do you use?" she asked, waving a hand at the products before her.

He looked at the options, then reached out and grabbed one and put it in the cart. "Now, I need coffee filters."

"Aisle four." She reversed course and started back in the direction they'd come, formulating a plan to get Tate into bed. They had to take his purchases back to his place, then she'd make her move. Just thinking about it had her body humming. Hopefully, Tate was better in bed than Howey Kent had been. It'd be a disappointment if he wasn't—a big one.

She cut down aisle four and pointed to his choices.

He picked one and placed it in the cart. "What's next?" She was in a hurry to get his shopping done so she could get to the next step—seducing Tate Donnelly.

Chapter Fourteen

It surprised Tate that Carrie had suggested stopping by his place to drop off his purchases since nothing he'd bought was perishable.

"Do you want to come inside?" he asked, sure she'd say no. Again, she shocked him. "Yes. I'd love to see your place."

"Okay," he said, reaching in the backseat to grab the bags, then opening his door to get out. By the time he came around the front of his Jeep, Carrie was waiting at his front door. She was acting weird, which sent his equilibrium off.

He quickly unlocked the door and allowed her to enter, hoping he hadn't left the place too much of a mess. Once inside, he went to put his groceries away and then came back to find Carrie standing in the living room looking nervous. "Is something wrong? Since we left the mart, you've been acting strange."

"No. Nothing's wrong."

Tate frowned. "Are you sure?"

She shifted from one foot to the other and pulled at the hem of her shirt. She clearly was anxious about something. He could see it in her mannerisms.

"You can tell me the truth. We're friends, aren't we?"

"Friends," she repeated, her cheeks taking on a pinkish tinge.

Jerri Drennen

"What the hell is going on, Carrie? Spit it out. It isn't like you to not be honest with me."

She swallowed repeatedly, then looked him in the eye. "It's been a long time," she said, then stopped and looked away.

"A long time for what?" Tate hadn't a clue what she was trying so hard to say. It wasn't like her not to be blunt and to the point. Not until now. Whatever this was, was difficult for her.

"I just thought since we were both single and…"

Now, he felt stupid because he had no idea what she was getting at.

"Yes. We are that. So?"

Tate stared at her, running her words around in his head. It was like a word jumble. *Single. Long time.*

Whoa. Wait a minute. Was she trying to suggest they sleep together? Have sex? What if he was wrong? She'd smack him from one end of town to the other. He needed her to say it. Otherwise, this conversation wasn't going anywhere.

"Would you like to elaborate further?" he asked, hoping she'd just say what she wanted.

She sighed, clearly getting frustrated with him.

"It would be completely up to you, of course."

Ugh. You are going to have to come out and ask, Carrie. I'm not moving an inch until you do.

"What is completely up to me? I don't understand."

"Forget it. Let's get going." She started for the door.

Boy, had he screwed this up. He raced to catch her, grabbing her arm before she reached out to open the door. "I'm sorry if I said something wrong." He drew her close enough that her breath tickled his neck and caused goose bumps to erupt over his body.

118

"No, it's my fault. I was being stupid."

"You're not stupid. You are bright and beautiful." The last part came out on its own. He hadn't meant to say it, even if it was true. She was stunning and she didn't seem to know it.

She grabbed him by the shoulders and pulled him down to cover his lips with hers, the instant electricity causing his brain to misfire. He wrapped his arms around her waist and drew her in close, the warmth and feel of her drowning him from further control. Tate was lost and happy to be. He deepened the kiss, his tongue teasing at the seam of her lips, applying pressure until she allowed him inside her mouth.

Then as passion flared, he backed her up to the sofa, thinking that was the closest place to continue. He broke contact long enough to ease her down, her eyes gleaming with desire. This woman was going to cause him trouble—the good kind.

Before joining her, he unbuttoned his shirt and shrugged it off, her gaze darkening. That only ignited a fire in his belly, and he moved to cover her, his lips melding into hers, his tongue forcing its way into her sweetness and mingling with hers. She moaned, and Tate allowed his fingers to roam up her side, exploring her firm yet pliant breast. Then on a mission, his mouth left hers and trailed down her neck, gliding over her collarbone, while his hands worked on the buttons of her shirt.

When the last one was free, he shoved the material away and gazed down at her white lacy bra. She was perfect in every way, and he wanted to stay in this moment and just admire her.

She squirmed beneath him and dipped her head into

the hollow of his neck and sucked on the skin, reigniting a fire. He worked at the button and zipper of her jeans, getting both unfastened. With an ardent hunger, he tugged the pants down over her hips and off, her panties following. He wanted to bury himself deep inside her but first he wanted to explore her body, give her pleasure before he got to his own. Her bra had a front clasp and he made quick work of getting rid of it. He took a nipple into his mouth and suckled, pleased at the moan he received, then he gave the other attention, causing her to arch up to his mouth. His hand snaked down her stomach and slid between her legs, teasing the flesh, causing her to groan in anticipation. He worked his way down her ribcage, nibbling at her skin, excited to cause goose bumps to form all over her body.

This was agonizing to a part of his anatomy. He couldn't wait, he tore open the condom he'd retrieved and rolled it onto his cock. He moved up to take her mouth in his and he plunged deep inside her, the heat surrounding him almost his undoing.

He counted to five, regaining his control, then slowly started to move, her hips meeting him thrust for thrust until he felt her clench and spasm, causing his own release.

Sated and exhausted, he dropped off to her side, trying to get his heart rate to slow. A minute or two passed until he felt the weight of the sofa shift. She'd left without saying a word.

****

Carrie reached for her clothes that were scattered around the couch, afraid to look at Tate, embarrassed by how out of control he'd made her feel. No man had ever done this to her before and it overwhelmed her, made her self-conscious. Did he think she was unsophisticated? Too small-town? *God.* She had no clue and was afraid to look at him—to see if he was disappointed.

Tears welled in her eyes, and she had to get a handle on her emotions before he noticed. "Where's your bathroom?" she asked, angry that her voice cracked.

"Down the hall on the left," he said, reaching out his hand to touch her. "Are you okay, Carrie?"

She didn't answer, just dashed to the bathroom, slamming the door behind her. What must he think? He gave her something no other had. An experience that she could never have imagined, and yet she ran away from him. She wouldn't blame him if he never talked to her again. Thought she was a lunatic.

A torrent of tears ran down her cheeks, and with anger, she wiped them away, too mortified to breathe. She quickly dressed, then sat on the toilet and squeezed her eyes shut.

A knock at the door made her jerk.

"Carrie, are you okay?"

What was she going to say? No? Tate wouldn't understand what she was feeling. Hell, she really didn't comprehend it herself. It was all so uncharacteristic. She'd always been able to handle herself, keep a level head, but this experience changed everything. Mind-blowing would have been a tepid word for what had happened.

Now, she didn't know how to act with him. The more she thought about it, the angrier she became. How could something so profound become so strangely upsetting to her? One thing she did know, she couldn't stay in the bathroom forever, no matter how much she wanted to. She had to buck it up and face him, at least long enough to say she had to go. She needed time to pull herself together and she couldn't do that in his presence.

The man was too distracting—too sexy. Just picturing him naked made her body respond. This was juvenile. She was acting like a teenager with her first crush, and if Tate knew, he'd probably laugh at her. All because they'd shared something spectacular for her and he'd seemed less than enthusiastic about it.

She shook the thought and opened the bathroom door to find Tate hovering nearby, a concerned look on his face.

"Is everything okay?" he asked, taking hold of her hand.

She instantly tugged it away, shocked by the current that shot up her arm. The man had ruined her. Made her reactive, and she didn't like it one bit.

"Did I do something wrong?" His face was masked now with worry.

Did you do anything wrong? I wish. If he had, she wouldn't feel so inadequate at that moment.

"I need to get home to take Molly out." She started toward the front door.

Before she could reach it, he grabbed her arm and turned her around to face him. "I did something that upset you, Carrie. Please just tell me what it was."

"You didn't do anything wrong, Tate. Like I said, I have to get to Emily's so Molly doesn't pee on the floor. She's not used to the house, and she might think it's okay if she has to go. Can you take me there, now?"

"Of course. Let's go."

In the SUV, she faced the window, her nerves in a jumble. She could only imagine what Tate was thinking. *This girl is one crazy bitch.* And, at the moment, he'd be right. This wasn't rational, sane, or logical, and she had no idea why she'd reacted like this.

He pulled into Emily's driveway, and she went for the door handle.

"Thanks for your help today," he said, his voice now guarded. "I really appreciate it either though we didn't learn anything at the mart."

She shrugged. "I'll see you." Then she got out and walked up the walkway, wanting so badly to turn back to look at him, but she couldn't. She was too afraid of what she'd see in his expression. Probably a look of total dismay, him wondering why in the hell he ever slept with her, and she couldn't blame him one bit.

Chapter Fifteen

Tate kicked the sheets on his bed away, too pent up to sleep. Carrie's clear contempt for him after the most amazing experience he'd had crushed his ego. He had no idea what he'd done wrong. He only knew that their romp had left a bad taste in her mouth—so bad in fact that she refused to even talk to him. Had it been that terrible for her? That was his thinking. Up until her, he'd had no complaints, so what had he done wrong?

He swallowed hard and got out of bed. Sleep would be futile. He might as well work. He still hadn't done the research on that judge.

He padded down the hall in his boxers and stepped into his office. He quickly turned on his computer then retraced his steps out the door to the kitchen to make some coffee. The plastic bags he'd unloaded were still sitting on the counter where he'd left them.

He reached inside a cabinet to get the coffee filters he'd bought then went to fill the pot with water. While it was brewing, he headed back to the office and sat down at his desk, quickly typing in his password. Bringing up his search engine, he punched in the judge's name and scanned the entries, one catching his eye. Wife, Maureen on the transplant list. Her heart was failing, and she was desperate to find a donor. The boxes at the dead men's houses flashed like a neon sign in his head.

Christ Almighty. Could it be what he was thinking it

could be? More importantly, did the judge know what was going on? If he did, presiding over that court case was not only unethical, but it was also downright criminal.

What he wouldn't give to be able to talk this through with Carrie, see if what he was thinking was even possible. But after this afternoon, he wasn't sure she'd ever speak to him again. The thought alone left an empty feeling inside him. Just being with her seemed to uplift him, even when they weren't really doing anything at all. He simply loved spending time with her. Now, that was in jeopardy.

Damn it all to hell and back.

He refused to think that way. He was going to make things right, even if he had to force her to sit down and tell him in detail what he'd done wrong. She'd seemed really into the sex, moaned and whimpered and…had he somehow hurt her? If that were the case, he'd kick his own ass. One way or the other, he was going to find out and make it right. He was stuck in Kendall, and she was the only bright spot in his days. Tate refused to lose that over a sexual encounter that had somehow gone awry.

That decided, he walked back to the kitchen and poured himself a mug of coffee. As he sipped the hot liquid, he stared out the window, the quiet serenity not going unnoticed. In D.C., sirens were always blaring, the lights of the city shining into his apartment, a place so tiny he could barely turn around. Here, in this small town, he rented a two-bedroom house with an office for pennies of what his apartment had cost him in D.C.

Tate continued to stare outside, noting the leaves from all the oak trees covered the slightly browning grass around them—fall was now in full swing. Everyone in his neighborhood had put up their Halloween decorations, a week away, some people having gone full horrorfest in their yards. Growing up, this had been his and Mia's favorite holiday, and he smiled at those long-forgotten memories.

He took another drink of coffee, picturing himself, his sister, and her husband taking his niece trick-or-treating, the child dressed in a princess costume. He could see her angelic face lighting up as she filled her Jack-o'-lantern with candy. Maybe someday he'd even take his own children. The thought brought him back to Carrie. She'd be a great mother since she was so good with animals.

"What in the world are you thinking, Tate?" Marrying someone and having babies was the last thing he needed. He was here to get his career back on track, not fantasize about having a family. Where had happily-ever-after gotten his mother? A drunken stupor on numerous occasions. He certainly didn't want that. Yet, how often did a spouse die? Steven Donnelly had been his mother's world and when he passed, her very existence came to a screeching halt and her children paid the price twice. Losing their father and their mother at the same time. She wasn't dead then, but she might as well have been. Her mothering skills had suffered greatly, and Tate never wanted to love someone so much that grief caused his own downhill spiral.

He brushed off the thought and dumped the rest of his coffee in the sink. He was going to try to go back to sleep. In the morning, he'd fix everything with Carrie, then they could go back to trying to unravel this mystery with the judge and that genetic testing company. But he needed a rested mind to do that.

As he headed back to his bedroom, the doorbell rang. He glanced at the clock on the living room wall and saw that it was getting close to midnight. Who the hell would be coming by his house at this time of night?

He rushed to get a pair of jeans to put on. Maybe it was Carrie. Could she be here to tell him how sorry she was about what had happened earlier? That would be the best-case scenario.

He jumped into the pants and was zipping them up as he reached the door. He removed the chain lock and opened the door. Not Carrie but the one woman he never wanted to see again. She stood ogling him since he hadn't put on a shirt.

"What are you doing here?" he said in an accusatory tone. This lady screwed him big-time and he wasn't talking about the time spent in bed. She'd ruined his career—made him have to leave the job he loved more than just about everything. The only thing more important to him was Mya.

"I miss you so much, baby. Aren't you going to invite me in?" She reached out to try and touch him, but he stepped back.

"No!" He scowled at her, thinking of slamming the door in her face.

She pouted. "You're still mad. I never meant for any of this to happen, Tate. I'm sorry. What can I do to make it up to you?"

"You can't. Now, turn around and go home before you have the media down here causing me more trouble."

"I can't leave. We love each other. I don't care who knows it."

The woman was delusional, and he was losing his

patience with her. "I don't feel anything for you, Rita. Zero. Zilch. Nothing. All I ever felt was sorry for you. Go back to your husband and find something else to occupy your time."

"You don't mean that, baby. I know you don't. What if I told you I asked John for a divorce? Would that change things?"

"No, it wouldn't change a damn thing. Now, I have to work in the morning. Goodbye, and good luck." He then closed the door and walked to his bedroom. He prayed that she'd do what he told her to, go back to Washington, D.C., because the last thing he needed now was her hanging around to fuck his life up further.

****

Carrie knew Emily was right, that she wasn't thinking clearly about what had happened. That she'd been overanalyzing their sexual encounter, and her imagining Tate's lack of response to what they shared. She knew he had way more experience in the bedroom than she had, obvious to them both. That only made her feel worse about her lack of control. The whole thing made her want to crawl in a hole.

Whatever made her think sleeping with him would be a good idea? It just made her feel like a lovesick, ignorant fool.

She covered her face with her hands, a sinking feeling taking hold.

"Stop what you are thinking, Carrie. You are being way too hard on yourself." Emily pried Carrie's hands from her cheeks.

"You can't say that. You weren't there."

Emily frowned. "I don't get why you are so upset. You just told me you had the best sex you've ever had, and you are mortified by it? Why? You can't possibly know what Tate was thinking."

"I know, but…"

Emily raised her hand. "No buts. Stop with the recriminations. It's all in your mind."

Carrie shook her head. Her best friend was trying to help. Torturing herself was stupid. It wasn't doing anything but causing more insecurity. That was the last thing she needed.

"Okay. I'm done going over this. You could be right. Can we just drop the subject, please?"

"Yes, we can. Now, eat your breakfast before it gets cold."

Carrie picked at her scrambled eggs, not at all hungry. She had to get over this mood she was in since it was a waste of time. She had more important things to worry about. There was a target on her back because of Doug's death and that was more dire than what Tate thought of her.

"I have to get to work. Will you be okay?" Emily stood next to the door.

Carrie gave her friend a reassuring smile. "I'll be fine. Have a good day."

After she'd gone, Carrie gathered up the dishes, rinsed them and placed them in the dishwasher right as Molly nudged her leg and looked up at her with those huge, liquid brown eyes. "I know, girl. I'll get ready to take you."

She walked to the front door to retrieve the leash and slipped on her shoes. She didn't plan to change her life because of a bunch of bullies.

Outside, she took in a breath of fresh air and started down the sidewalk, Molly taking the lead, stopping here and there to sniff at anything of interest. As they were rounding the corner, her attention was instantly drawn to the jeep headed her way. It was Tate. Maybe he wouldn't stop.

She continued down the walkway, trying to look straight ahead. She wasn't ready to talk to him yet, though she wasn't overemotional about things anymore.

"Carrie," he called, stopping her in her tracks. So much for him driving by. No way could she avoid him now.

She turned to find him pulled up next to the sidewalk, his window down, a look of apprehension on his face. He was as unsure as she was. That went a long way to relieve her mind.

"Hello," she said, not sure what else to say.

"I want to tell you that I was sorry about anything I did to upset you yesterday. That was the last thing I wanted to do."

She drew closer to the vehicle. What was *he* sorry about? She should be the one apologizing. "No, Tate, I'm sorry. I don't know what came over me. I was being irrational. Stupid really."

He shook his head. "Not stupid at all. You were bothered by something I did, and I want you to be able to tell me when I overstep. I feel like I hurt you in some way and I never want to do that again."

"Can we just forget it happened?"

"I don't think I can, Carrie."

She slumped, not knowing what to do next. He refused to forget about her crazy reaction. How could they fix this if he wouldn't put it behind them?

"Yesterday, with you, meant a lot to me. It was quite wonderful. You, though, clearly didn't have the same experience and I'm sorry about that. Maybe you could tell me what I did wrong, and next time it could be better for you."

Wait, what? Her jaw dropped. He was telling her that he felt like she had about their sexual encounter. Why hadn't she been able to see that? Was he lying to make her feel better?

She studied his face. No. He looked sincere about what he'd told her.

"I think we both misinterpreted each other's reactions. I too thought it was amazing."

His eyes widened. "So, you thought I didn't?"

"I don't have the experience that you clearly do, Tate. I felt very inadequate."

"Not at all, Carrie. Can we please both start this day over? I have so much to talk to you about."

She smiled, feeling relieved. Next time she allowed her mind to go crazy, she was going to stop herself. "I need to finish walking Molly. Then we can talk."

"I'll go grab us a coffee and come back. Does that sound good?"

"Sounds perfect. See you in a few."

Carrie watched as he pulled away, the tension in her body now lifted. She took off down the sidewalk, feeling good. On the last turn back to Emily's, a truck barreled by and pulled into her friend's driveway. Both of Doug's brothers got out of the cab, waiting for her.

She swallowed a lump of apprehension as she neared the truck. No way would she make it to the door. She was going to have to deal with them.

"What do you want?" she asked the youngest, who was closest to her.

"You need to get what's coming to you, bitch.

Mama is crying her eyes out. Nobody makes my mama cry."

"I didn't touch Doug. Leave me alone."

"Well, that ain't exactly true, is it? I watched you slap my brother in the face the same day he ended up dead. The alibi of yours don't mean shit to me. Just because that old lady said you were home, doesn't mean you were."

What was she supposed to say to that? The man was not going to listen to reason. Nothing she said would change his mind. It was set on believing she was Doug's killer.

"I didn't like Doug. That much is true, but I'd never harm him. I don't even own a gun."

Both brothers scowled at her. "That best friend of yours does."

"You think I'd take Emily's weapon to kill your brother? Are you insane?"

"Don't fucking call me insane, bitch. You should be in jail right now, or better yet, dead."

Those words sent a cold chill through Carrie. Were they telling her that they wanted to kill her? She needed to get out of here now.

A squealing of tires had her turning to see Tate pulling up to the curb and jumping out to come around to get to her. His face was masked in anger. "Get out of here, now," he said, coming to block her. "How many times do you have to be told that Carrie had nothing to do with your brother's death?"

The two backed away but didn't leave. "Why don't you mind your own business, boy."

"Boy," Tate repeated, fisting his hands at his side. "Do you want to see this boy punch the shit out of both of you?"

The brothers' eyes widened, then they shuffled to the truck. "Next time, little girlie. You wait and see." They jumped into the cab of the truck and pulled out of the driveway, squealing their tires as they took off down the street.

"You okay?" He brushed her arm with his hand.

Carrie had no idea if she was or not. They'd threatened her life, and now she'd be watching her back until Doug's real killer got brought to justice.

Chapter Sixteen

Tate waited for Carrie to put Molly back in the house, sipping the coffee he'd gone to get. Thank God the line at the café had been short and he'd been able to get in and out in only a few minutes. Who knew what would have happened?

Doug's family was a blemish on the city of Kendall, and they'd be better off with one less of them to wreak havoc, though his murderer would have to be found.

Carrie stepped out the door and his heart rate hitched. No woman had ever made him feel so alive, and he wasn't sure how he should react. What did it mean? Had she become important to him—someone he cared about? Yes. He did care for her but was it more than that?

She opened the door to his Jeep, and he was immediately brought back to what he needed to do. To find out why those two men had the genetic testing kits in their homes and what that company did with their data.

Once she was inside and had secured her seat belt, Tate started the engine and eased away from the curb.

"I want to run some idea by you if that's okay?"

Her face instantly lit up. "I'm ready."

He loved this about her. She seemed interested in what he did.

"So, we now know that both Tripp and Chandler had those DNA kits, right? From the same company. We need to find out who they are and where the data goes."

"Okay. Where do we start?"

"I have my computer. We could go into the café and do an internet search. By the way, the judge in the Chandler case has a wife in ICU. She had a heart transplant."

"Are you serious?"

"I wish I wasn't. This is not going to bode well for him if what I'm thinking pans out."

"You mean if that heart came from Tripp?"

"Yeah. I mean, did he know where that heart was coming from? We need to find that out, too."

Tate pulled up in front of the café and the two got out and entered the restaurant, settling on a booth in the back.

Instead of sitting across from him, she slid in next to him, her nearness igniting a fire in his belly. *Tamp it down, Tate.*

"I want to see what you find." Her eyes lit up with excitement.

"Have you ever thought of investigative journalism?" he asked.

"Never but I am having fun with this."

"I can see that."

The waitress brought them both coffee, then left them alone.

Tate opened his computer and turned it on. He then typed in his passwords and brought up the search engine. He found the testing name and read over the info on the site. Kits were sent and then you returned the sample to them into the prepaid packaging. After the DNA was tested, the person would receive an email with results. Where were the tests done though? What lab? He couldn't find any info on that.

Carrie, too, was reading the page and frowned.

"What?" he asked.

"Does this place seem legit to you? I don't see the name of the lab where the work is done. Did I miss that?"

He couldn't believe she'd caught that too. He'd been doing this kind of thing for years and she picked it up just like that. "I saw that too. Something doesn't feel right with this. I'd love to see inside one of those boxes."

"Really? Are you suggesting we break into Vince's house, because if you are, I can do one better. Beth still has a key to his place. He refused to take it back."

"You think you could get it from her."

"I do. Let me run by the bank, ask her, and I'll be back in twenty minutes."

"That would be great. I'm going to go in and talk to my editor. Let him know what I'm working on and that I'll be out of the newspaper all day. I'll pick you up in front of the bank."

Carrie sucked down the last of her coffee, then rose, a gleam of mischief in her amazing eyes. The woman sent his heart racing again, especially when he thought about what she looked like naked. Curves in the right places. All real. So much better than those plastic women in D.C.. He watched her butt wiggle, and he squirmed on the booth seat. At the counter the waitress gave him a grin. She knew what he'd been staring at. He cleared his throat and loaded up his stuff. It was best to get out of there. He paid for the coffee and left, hoping Dennis wouldn't have a story he wanted Tate to cover. This adventure he and Carrie were about to undertake was starting to excite him. Hell, just being with her did that. But he couldn't wait to get into the dead man's house and see what they could find and hope they didn't get caught.

At the light, he turned into the lot area of the newspaper and parked. Inside, he walked straight to Dennis's office and stuck his head in. "You got anything you want me to cover?"

Dennis shook his head. "It's a pretty quiet day."

"Okay, good. I'm working on something big. At least, I think it is. I hope to have something to share with you in a few days."

His editor's eyes widened. "You can't give me a hint?"

"It's linked to the Tripp death."

"Go. Get me something good."

"All right. I'll get back to you as soon as I can."

Tate retraced his steps to the front door and left. Dennis had no idea how big this story could be, could blow the roof off the courthouse in Bailey and uncover something sinister.

He jumped in his SUV and headed for the bank. In all the time he'd been an investigative reporter he'd never broken into a property, but he and Carrie were about to do just that.

At the bank, he slid into a parking spot and cut the engine, glancing around, spotting the woman he despised entering the café. Why the hell hadn't she left town like he told her to? If she stayed more than a few days and that dastardly husband of hers showed up, everything would hit the fan.

****

Carrie had to admit that breaking and entering was exhilarating, though did having a key somehow excuse it? Probably not, but they were still going inside. The two reached the back door and she inserted the key into the lock and turned the knob. There was no turning back now. She and Tate were now breaking the law.

Carrie stepped inside and glanced around, the smell of dirty dishes and rotting garbage assailing her senses. Clearly the man had lived like a pig. Why hadn't his family asked to come clean it up?

She turned to Tate who too was looking at the sink that was filled with stacks of dishes, pans and glasses. "He obviously didn't have a cleaning lady."

"He worked as little as possible. I doubt he could afford one."

"We'd better hurry and get in and out before we catch something."

Just then a mouse scurried across the floor and disappeared into another room.

Carrie held onto the scream that wanted to escape. They needed to stay quiet, or the neighbors might call the cops. The last thing she needed was a felony on her record, especially after being questioned by the sheriff for murder.

The two found the living room and searched for the white box from the testing facility yet came up short. It was in the crime scene photos so where did it go?

"Do you think the sheriff could have taken it?" she asked Tate.

"Either that or someone was covering their tracks. Maybe they'd forgotten to take the box on the day Vince was murdered and came back to retrieve it later. They clearly weren't counting on pictures being taken since it looked like a natural death to begin with."

"So, what's next?" Suddenly, she was feeling defeated.

"We need to dig into that company further. Check out the hospital where Judge Brier's wife had the transplant. See if the two are connected in some way."

"Then let's get started."

He smiled at her, and it caused a strange sensation in the pit of her belly. This man was too distracting for his own good, and for hers as well.

They returned to the kitchen and left, locking the door behind them. Beth had told her to keep the key, that she didn't need it back. Carrie tucked it under the mat and followed Tate to his Jeep and jumped in. "Off to the hospital, then?" she asked, glancing over at him.

"Yes. Hopefully, they'll be able to give us some answers, though HIPPA laws may become a problem.

Do you want to stop at Emily's to take Molly out before we go?"

"Yes. Thanks for reminding me."

Carrie sat back, thinking she'd never known any other man as thoughtful as Tate. Everything about him was unique.

He pulled up in front of Emily's and she turned to him. "This shouldn't take long."

He popped his door. "I'll be nearby just in case Doug's family shows up again. You might want to tell the sheriff about what's going on or get a restraining order."

She shook her head. "I'm not going to let them bully me. They are all bark and no bite." Right after she'd said it, she remembered them throwing that rock through Emily's window. Hopefully, her friend would have talked to the sheriff, and he would speak to the Walshes about it. If not, then she'd have to move back to her own home to keep them from causing more damage.

Fifteen minutes later, the two were off again, on their way to the hospital outside of Bailey.

"I may have to go back home." Even the idea of that made Carrie nervous. She may appear tough to most people but being alone while the Walshes were on the warpath didn't sit well at all.

He glanced at her and frowned. "That's not a good idea, Carrie. You can't stay at your place alone."

"I didn't tell you that someone threw a rock through Emily's window the other night. I think we can both figure out who. I just can't put my best friend at risk. If anything ever happened to her..." The thought alone made her shiver.

"I see what you mean. I have a solution, then."

"Oh?"

"Yes. I'll come stay with you. On the couch, of course."

She turned to him, her eyes wide. "Wait, what?"

"I'm not taking no for an answer. After we get back, we'll go by and get Molly and you can tell Emily what's going on, then I'll pack a few things and that's that."

Chapter Seventeen

Tate couldn't say he was disappointed with this new predicament. Spending the night with Carrie was a dream come true, though he wouldn't push them sharing a bed. Everything that happened once they were alone would be on her terms. To add the cherry on top, Rita wouldn't be able to find him there.

In front of him, Carrie stood, key in hand, Molly at her feet. He'd been surprised how friendly the little girl was to him. He'd never had a pet before since he spent too many hours gone and he had no room. Which wouldn't be fair to any animal.

"Come on in." She stepped inside the door and allowed him inside. She then closed it and sent the bolt lock in place. When she turned to face him, Tate could tell she was anxious. He didn't want her to be.

"I want you to know, Carrie, that me being here is all about your safety. Okay?"

She smiled, then unleashed Molly, who took off down the hallway.

"What do we do next since we found out nothing at the hospital?"

He nodded. "That was a dead end, wasn't it? Then again, even if they knew something, would they have really implicated themselves?"

"So, what then? Do we give up?"

"Not a chance. I think I need to have a little talk with

the judge in question. Maybe he knows more about this than anyone since his wife could have been a recipient of Vince's organs."

Her beautiful eyes narrowed. "Are you just going to walk into his office and ask him?"

"I'm going to go and speak to him about the Adler case and hope he slips up and gives me something."

She frowned. "And you think you can make that happen?"

Tate grinned. "I do. Believe it or not, I'm a good investigative reporter, Carrie."

"So, then why are you in Kendall? Why aren't you in Washington, D.C. where you want to be?"

Shit. What was he going to say? He couldn't tell her the truth. Somehow, he knew she wouldn't be okay with that scenario, probably would never want to see him again, and he didn't want that. He loved having her around. She was a great sounding board, and she made his days in this tiny town doable. Without her, he'd lose his mind.

Who the hell was he kidding? He cared about her, more than he should and that was a death sentence in his mind. In some way, he had to keep his head. Love wasn't an option, especially when he planned to move back to D.C. as soon as possible. His career was there, and so was Mya. He couldn't allow his feelings for Carrie to cloud that.

"I was kicked to the curb by my paper. Hopefully, I can get picked up by another with the right buzz." It wasn't a lie, just a thin version of the truth.

Her face seemed to lose a bit of its color, why, Tate had no idea. She then turned and headed down the hall, following her dogs' path.

He'd clearly said something that had upset her. *What's wrong with you, asshole.* Best to leave her alone for a while.

He walked over to her couch and sat, then opened his computer bag and grabbed his laptop. He needed to find the judge's clerk's office hours, see if he couldn't be seen for a story. The sooner the better. This connection between this testing company and the judge could be the article of a lifetime. Black market organs. You have the money, we can find the donor. Dead or alive.

Jesus Christ. Just the thought of such a thing made him want to lose his lunch. The inhumanity was earth-shattering. What kind of evil doctor would condone such a thing? One that would *pay* if Tate had his way.

****

Carrie stepped into the kitchen and found Molly sitting in the spot where her water and food would've been. She rushed to get her bowls and filled one with kibble, the other with cold water. Immediately, Molly started to eat.

Tate's comments in the living room played on a loop in her head. And it needed to. He planned to leave when he had another job. She needed to get that through her head.

Emotion clogged her throat. Figures that the one and only time she put down her guard, this happened. She should have known this would end with her brokenhearted.

She shook her head. *Stop it. You are tougher than this. Just enjoy the time you have with him and then let go.*

With that, she walked to the refrigerator and grabbed a bottle of water. She'd never needed anyone before. She didn't need anyone now.

Her phone chirped and she glanced at her screen, not recognizing the number. Maybe it was a new client—someone she'd handed one of her cards out to.

Working would be a good thing right now.

She pressed answer, and said, "Hello."

"Is this Carrie Pruitt?"

"It is." The woman on the other end sounded distressed. She doubted it was a prospective client.

"I need to talk to you about Doug Walsh."

A chill raced across her body. "What about him?"

"I need to see you in person. Can we meet somewhere later today?"

Carrie didn't know what to say. Could it be some kind of trap to get her alone? Could the Walshes be orchestrating it?

"You can't tell me what it's about?"

"No. Not over the phone. Please. I need to speak with you."

How could Carrie say no. "Okay. Where do you want to meet?"

"There's a little café on Remer. Al's Diner. Could we meet there in an hour?"

"All right. I'll be there." Carrie ended the call. Now, to somehow get past Tate to have this little meet and greet. That wasn't going to be easy. She'd need to be covert, there and back. Maybe he wouldn't even notice that she was gone since he hadn't followed her into the kitchen.

God. This was going to be difficult. An idea hit her. She'd tell him she was going out to her garage to set up for a new client, and she'd promise to lock the door while inside.

She retraced her steps to the front, finding Tate sitting on the sofa, his laptop up, him writing down something on a notepad.

He smiled when he noticed her. "I have to run out to the garage and set up for a new client that just called for a shampoo and trim. I'll lock the door while I'm in there."

"Are you sure you don't want me to go with you?"

"No...no, you're busy. I promise I'll secure the door. No one will be able to get in."

"Okay. I'll see you when you get back."

Now, with that out of the way, her nerves returned. What if she was walking into a trap like she had first thought? Tate wouldn't even know she was gone.

Carrie couldn't think that way. Not now.

She took a cleansing breath and walked back to the kitchen to grab her phone. If she needed to, she'd call for help. Outside, she cut through her backyard and took off toward Main Street. She couldn't risk taking her truck. Tate would hear her leave. She was going to have to walk, and it would take her every bit of forty minutes to get to this diner—one she had never been to before. She spent most of her time at her favorite hangouts. Had never wandered past them in all the time she'd lived in Kendall.

To save time, she took a few alleyways that helped to get her to her destination sooner. At the entrance to the diner, she glanced at her phone and saw she'd arrived five minutes early.

Inside, she glanced around, not recognizing anyone. That was odd. She thought she knew just about everyone in town. But apparently not.

Carrie went to sit at a small table with two chairs.

She had no idea who she was waiting for. She could only hope that this woman knew her.

She ordered a coffee and waited. The handful of people who were there thankfully seemed to ignore her. That was a good thing. All she needed was for someone to say something about Doug and his murder.

The front door jingled and in walked a thin woman with dark-blonde hair, her features gaunt, her skin pale. She didn't look well at all.

The woman came toward Carrie and sat down in front of her.

She too ordered a coffee and after receiving her mug, sat back, studying Carrie. The woman seemed to be anguishing over how to start. Carrie would make it easier.

"I'm just going to come out and ask. What did you want to see me about?"

"My name is Diana Sherman. I went to high school with Doug. He raped me one night after a football game. I tried to tell people, but no one would listen. He and his family destroyed my life. I know that he had bothered you. My parents told me about it when I returned to town two weeks ago."

Carrie's mouth gaped. This was the last thing she expected to hear. "I'm so sorry you had to go through that."

"When you experience something so traumatic, you have PTSD whenever something triggers the memory."

"It must be horrible for you. I can't even imagine."

"It's been a nightmare, but I owe you an apology. I never dreamed my actions would cause you pain. I'm truly sorry."

Carrie didn't have a clue as to what the woman was

talking about. "I'm sorry. I'm not following you."

"I just wanted to tell you this before I go to the police station later. My mother asked me if I could go pick up something at the mart Thursday night."

Carrie swallowed hard, knowing now what was coming.

"He was there. He spotted me and I tried to get to my car. He caught me and dragged me to his truck. I just couldn't go through it again. I snapped. Since I'd left town, I always carried a gun in my purse. We fought over it, and it went off. I never wanted to kill him. It just happened. When I found out you had been questioned, I knew I had to tell you what happened before I turned myself in. Can you please forgive me for not coming to you sooner, for letting the Walshes think you'd killed him?"

Could she forgive her? Somehow, she knew she had to. The woman had been through too much not to understand.

Carrie reached across the table and squeezed her wrist. "Of course, I can. I'm sorry for what Doug and his family did to you."

Diana's eyes filled with tears, and Carrie could tell she was struggling to keep herself together.

"I must go. My parents are meeting me at the sheriff's office with an attorney. Thank you again for meeting with me and understanding." She rose and walked to the counter to pay for her coffee, then left.

Carrie sat back, taking everything in she'd just learned. Would she have done the same if the shoe had been on the other foot? She hoped so.

She drank the last of her coffee, then went to pay, finding out that Diana had already done so. "Thank you," she said, then walked out the door.

Once she was back on the walkway, she glanced at the time on her phone, instantly picking up her pace. If she didn't get moving, Tate would know she was gone and come looking for her, and she was sure he'd let her know how stupid it was to meet someone, not knowing who.

Chapter Eighteen

Tate tried to get comfortable for the tenth time but Carrie's sofa wasn't long enough to accommodate his body. His feet hung over the arm and caused the back of his heels to cramp. Frustrated, he sat up and scratched the stubble on his chin. So, he wasn't going to get any sleep tonight, or longer if he stayed here.

He rose and walked to the kitchen to make a pot of coffee. If he couldn't rest, he might as well write the piece that Dennis sent him on about the city council meeting that one of the other reporters didn't have time to write, though Tate had the man's summary notes.

He glanced around and couldn't find a coffeemaker. Didn't everyone have one?

He opened a cabinet and found a jar of instant coffee. He didn't even think they still made the stuff. The kettle was on the stove, and he found that it was already filled with water. He switched on the burning, then went to find a cup. In another cupboard there were three mismatched mugs. Carrie clearly lived a minimalist lifestyle. Hell, maybe this was all she could afford. Would she be offended if he bought her a few things? Knowing her, probably. Though, if he brought his coffeemaker over while he was here, he doubted she'd object. Maybe he'd also buy an air mattress so he could get at least a few hours of sleep.

A creak of a floorboard made him turn. Carrie stood

in the doorway, wearing a snug-fitting pink T-shirt and a pair of striped drawstring pajama pants. She looked at him, then rubbed her eyes.

"Did I wake you?"

She smiled. "That's okay. What are you doing up?"

He wasn't going to tell her the truth. She'd feel bad and that was the last thing he wanted. "I remembered my editor sent me notes on an article I need to write by tomorrow morning." Not really a lie, though he didn't need it until late afternoon.

"I have to tell you something." She shifted from one foot to the other. "Something that will come to your attention tomorrow at work."

Tate frowned. What could Carrie know that he didn't? "Okay. What's that?"

"You know when I told you I was out in my garage setting up and grooming a dog?"

"Yeah."

"I lied to you. I knew you wouldn't allow me to go if I told you the truth."

A tingle of apprehension raced up his back. "Go where, Carrie?" His words came out with more force than he'd intended. But he was angry that she might have done something that could have put her life in danger.

"I got a call from a woman who insisted we meet. It was in public. People were around. I was safe while I was there."

"There where?"

"A little diner off the beaten path. I'd never been there before. Didn't recognize anyone inside. Which was a good thing because of what the Walshes were telling people about me."

"So, who did you meet with?"

"Diana Sherman. She was raped by Doug while in high school. She told me she'd gone to the mart to pick up something for her parents and that Doug attacked her again, fought over a gun in her purse, and it'd gone off. You know what happened next."

Tate's mouth gaped. What a story, one he'd need to write about, but only after he spoke with the sheriff to confirm it all.

"How did you get to this diner? I didn't hear your truck leave."

She fidgeted again. "I walked."

"You walked? With the Walshes on the loose. You walked off a beaten path?"

She stepped closer to him. "I know. I shouldn't have done it, but I knew you wouldn't let me go and I had to. The woman was so persistent."

"Okay, I get that. You are just lucky you didn't have a run-in with any of Doug's family. They seem to be everywhere these days."

She nodded. "I know and I'm sorry, but at least now we know how Doug died. I want to help Diana in some way. I, of all people, know how horrible that bunch can be, and Doug didn't rape me. Though, I might have been had you not shown up in my garage the day we first met. Clearly, the man is capable of anything."

Tate had to agree. Doug Walsh was a despicable man and, frankly, the world was a better place without him in it.

"What do you think you can do?" he asked, not sure there was anything she could do at this point. "It sounded like it was self-defense, but she didn't report the shooting right away. That could sway public opinion. The police could get her for leaving the scene of a crime and possible murder if a jury didn't believe her story."

"I get that. But I want to be there if she needs me to tell my own story about Doug and his harassment. It might help her case in some way."

Tate smiled. Carrie was a good person. So unlike Rita. That woman was a shark, one he planned to avoid as long as she stayed in town. He should come clean to Carrie about her, but he just wasn't ready to reveal that transgression. For whatever reason, he knew she wouldn't think what he did was acceptable. Hell, he didn't. If he could take it all back, he would in a heartbeat.

"I'll let you get back to writing your story. I'll see you in the morning."

He didn't want her to leave, though it was probably for the best. It was hard to be so close to her and not want to pull her into his arms and kiss her until all the shit in his life disappeared. Yet, that wasn't what she wanted, and he wouldn't ever force anything on her. She had become too important to him.

The kettle whistled and he went to pour water into a mug and stirred in some coffee crystals, sure this wasn't going to be his favorite cup of java.

He took the mug into the living room and sat in front of his laptop, quickly reading over the notes he'd gotten for the article. Thirty minutes later, the story was written, and his coffee barely touched. He emailed the article to his editor and then turned off his computer. Now, he was going to have to try to get some sleep or tomorrow was going to be rough, especially if he ran into Rita Philips again.

****

Carrie woke and rolled over to see what time it was,

surprised that it was almost eight o'clock. She'd had a rough night. Could barely sleep, especially after her talk with Tate. She'd heard him in the kitchen, watched as he put on the kettle. The man was the best-looking male specimen she'd ever seen. He made her skin tingle just staring at him, remembering what he'd felt like inside her. Nothing could even come close to the experience. Yet, he hadn't even tried to kiss her since.

Did he have the opposite experience?

She squeezed her eyes closed, feeling so inadequate. What did he expect? She barely had any knowledge when it came to sex. One other man in her past, a few years after she'd moved to Kendall, before Doug started chasing men away.

She rose from bed. If Tate didn't want her, he didn't want her. There was nothing she could do about that. Besides, he was leaving when his chance came and that could happen if this genetic testing story panned out. This was big and she was sure he could tell it in a way that would give him country-wide exposure, enough to draw the right people to him and his talent. Then he'd be gone. Best to realize that now.

She walked to her bathroom and opened the door, shocked to find Tate pulling the shower curtain back, beads of water glistening on his amazing body.

Her jaw slackened and she stood ogling him, unable to move, to speak, to catch her breath.

He smiled, revealing his sparkling white teeth and everything around her seemed to disappear. The man couldn't be any more alluring, so appealing to her senses.

She swallowed hard, afraid to say anything.

He reached out for her arm and pulled her into him, the feel of his slick body igniting a charge in her belly.

His lips swooped down onto hers, causing her brain to misfire. Then, he walked her backward, his naked thigh between her legs, rear-end bumping up against the sink. His hands encircled the small of her back, drawing her up against his hard cock. She tore her mouth from his and quickly stripped off her clothes, wanting his naked, slick skin next to her own.

Then her mouth met his again, his tongue sliding in to capture hers, his hand cupping her breast, teasing the nipple. She moaned against his mouth, her need so powerful she thought she'd explode. With swiftness, he nudged her legs apart and plunged a finger inside her wet heat, causing her to buck forward. His mouth left hers and dipped to her breast, sucking her nipple into his mouth, and she laced her hand through his hair and relished the pleasure. His mouth captured hers again for a soul-numbing kiss, one that made her head spin. When he drew back, he looked at her, his eyes so filled with desire. He did want her. She could see it.

He reached down and grabbed his wallet from his pants and extracted a foil packet and tore it open with his teeth, then rolled it onto his cock and drove deep inside her, the pressure causing her to immediately coil and come hard. He barely had to touch her to make her explode.

Slow and with purpose, he started to move, each measured thrust reigniting a sensation that ended with them both coming, together, so intense that they both almost slid off the sink edge. He caught her and they both started to laugh, then held each other tight, neither wanting to let go.

When Carrie finally did look up, Tate was staring at her, a look that made her suddenly feel self-conscious.

"What?" she said, unsure of what he was thinking.

"Nothing," he said, his voice huskier than normal.

"No, really. What were you thinking? I want to know."

"I was thinking I wish I could stay like this all day."

She smiled. "Why can't we?"

"Because you threw a story in my lap last night and I need to follow it up."

"Always the instigative reporter."

"How about I use those skills later to do some research on your body? There are avenues I haven't even begun to explore yet."

She had to giggle, though the thought caused a tightening in her core. "You're on. How long until you can get back?"

"Give me a couple of hours and I'll be all yours."

"Can I hold you to that?"

"Absolutely." He moved away from her but then came back and kissed her hard on the mouth. "Don't go anywhere. I want you here when I get back."

"I'll be in bed waiting."

He groaned. "Woman. You are going to drive me crazy."

"That's the goal. Now, get going so you can return."

Chapter Nineteen

Tate whistled as he jumped from his vehicle, on his way in to speak to the sheriff about the update on Doug Walsh's death. Hopefully, everything would come out about what had happened and that would take the pressure off Carrie. The Walshes would then leave her alone. Yet, if that were the case, he wondered if she'd want him to go back to his place. After what they'd just shared, he hoped not. He wanted to spend as much time with her as possible, preferably in bed. Sex with Carrie was the most incredible experience he'd ever had, and he wanted to explore that further.

Inside the police station, he walked up to the window and smiled at Emily, who waved, then handed him a sheet of paper. He scanned over it, seeing that it was a notice to the press on the Walsh murder and indeed named his killer.

"Is it true that this Diana talked to Carrie yesterday?" Emily asked him.

Tate nodded. "I didn't know myself until late last night. She snuck out to meet with her. Do the Walshes know about this turn of events?"

"Yes. The sheriff talked to them this morning. Diana is lucky she's in our custody. They are out for blood."

"Are they going to apologize to Carrie for terrorizing her?"

Emily snorted. "Don't count on it. The Walshes

156

don't say they're sorry for anything."

Tate shook his head. "Kendall would be a much better place if that family left town."

"From your mouth to God's ears."

"Okay, well, I'll talk to you soon."

"Tell Carrie to call me when she can."

"Will do."

He turned and left, glad all this with the Walshes and Carrie was over. Now, he had to go write the story, get it in to his editor and then get back to her. All the things he planned to do to her warmed his skin and caused his cock to jump. The woman was going to drive him nuts.

He drove to the paper and went inside, said hello, and walked straight to his cubicle. The computer was booted up and ready. He took out the press release Emily had given him and skimmed the paper again. Then he started to write, trying to give a perspective on the woman, using what Carrie had told him last night. He wanted the story to be sympathetic to her since Doug Walsh was the town bully and a rapist, from what Diana had revealed. If he was again trying to attack her, what was she supposed to do—let him? No. Doug Walsh was a lowlife and got what he deserved.

After spellchecking everything, he sent it to the copyeditor and printed out a photocopy for Dennis to read to okay publication.

He grabbed the paper once it was printed and walked to Dennis's office and knocked on the frame of the open door.

His editor signaled for him to come in, since he was on the phone. He pointed to the chair and Tate sat.

"Okay. Thanks for calling." He put the phone back in its cradle. "That was a source over in Bailey.

According to him, Judge Briers' wife passed away last night from organ rejection. You are going to need to follow up on that story today."

Tate's mind was spinning a mile a minute. Why had the organ been rejected? Could it have been from Vince, who clearly drank to excess? Would that be something that would cause a problem with the organ itself? He clearly needed to find out.

"I'll get right on that." He handed Dennis his article. "I need to know if you can run this in tomorrow's paper?"

His editor read over the story, his eyes widening, a flicker of a smile crossing over his lips.

"How did you find this out? I haven't heard a word about it."

"I had an inside source."

"You had an inside source. I've had writers here for ten years who don't have contacts like this. I'm glad I hired you, Donnelly. Scandal or no scandal. Did you send this to Chip yet?"

"I did."

"Good. This story will be on the front page tomorrow. Good job, Tate. Now, go get me this story on the judge's wife."

Tate rose from his chair. "Yes, sir."

Now, he was going to have to call Carrie. Here, he'd wanted to spend the day with her and he couldn't. This lead was big. If that transplant came from Tripp, and the judge knew it, he'd had a hand in his own wife's death. Tate needed to find out quickly if that was the case, even if that meant not being in Carrie's arms.

Outside in his vehicle, he pressed her number and waited, getting no answer. *Crap.* He'd keep trying while heading to Bailey.

Forty-minutes later, he stepped into the municipal building, still unable to reach Carrie. Down the hallway were a row of offices on either side, at the end, the judge's chamber. Hopefully, Tate could talk to one of his clerks, see if they had any information of his wife's passing.

He stepped into an open door; the woman at the desk looked up, her light, amber eyes expressing interest. He'd use that to get her to open up. "Hello. How are you today?"

"Fine. Yourself?"

"I'm doing good. Thank you. I'm here to see if the judge is available."

Her face changed immediately, those same eyes clouding with tears. "He's not in today and probably won't be for the remainder of the week. His wife passed away last night."

"I'm so sorry. Could I ask you to give him my number? I really need to talk to him when he gets a chance."

"Of course." She handed him a sticky note and a pen.

Tate wrote down his name and number and handed it back to her.

He then thanked her and left. Hopefully, the man would call him. If not, he'd have to try another route. One way or another, he'd get to the truth. He prayed it wasn't as bad as he thought.

****

Carrie couldn't believe what this woman sitting across from her had revealed. Emotional turmoil filled her with a sickening feeling—like she was drowning.

Tate had had an affair with this lady and lost everything because of it. And, to add insult to injury, she was in love with him and wanted Carrie to know that. Wanted her to step aside and let her have him.

"Are you going to do the right thing?" The woman named Rita's eyes practically shot sparks at her.

Anger overtook Carrie's disappointment. This woman had no hold over Tate, wasn't even free since she was married to a congressman in Washington. That alone made Carrie more defiant. "I believe this is up to Tate," she said. "And your husband as well."

The blonde huffed and tucked a strand of her short bob behind her ears, pursing her bright red lips. The woman was pissed but Carrie didn't care. She might be questioning her relationship with Tate right now, but she wasn't about to tell this woman that. Rita could keep thinking Carrie didn't care about him sleeping with a married woman. She did, yet this woman wasn't getting that information from her.

"You have no idea what is going on in my marriage," Rita said in a tone that was meant to intimidate her.

"I couldn't care less. Now, I have things to do. I'm going to ask you to leave."

Rita's jaw clenched and she snarled at Carrie, then reluctantly rose and started for the door.

Carrie followed, still fuming at the woman's gall. On the stoop, Rita turned to face her. "I could make life for you miserable. You might want to rethink your stance here."

"So, you are threatening me now?"

"I'm just suggesting it's in your best interest to tell Tate you no longer want to see him."

"You're a real piece of work." Carrie got ready to close the door. "Now, get out of here and don't come back."

While taking the step down, she said over her shoulder, "I'm not leaving town alone. Be forewarned."

Carrie slammed the door, then squeezed her eyes shut and fisted her hands at her side. She couldn't remember the last time she was this angry. All because of Tate. Hell, even Doug and his family hadn't stirred such ire.

Tears blinded her vision, emotion clogging her throat. How had she allowed this man to weasel his way into her heart, a man who wasn't worthy? Cheating was a deal breaker for her. You couldn't trust a man who would do that, and she needed that to be confident in someone. Tate Donnelly wasn't the man she'd thought he was, and she had to push him away, even if it meant crushing her state of mind.

She stalked from the door as her phone rang. For some reason she knew it was Tate again. He'd been trying to call her since Rita came to her door, so sophisticated, so unlike herself. Carrie had instantly felt intimidated. Yet, when she asked to come in and revealed what she had about Tate, Carrie was no longer daunted—only disgusted by her. Here was a woman married to one man insisting another belonged to her. Who did that? Typical D.C. bullshit. Not that she knew a single thing about the city or people who lived there.

She cringed and picked up her phone. It was Tate. What was she going to do? If he didn't get an answer, he'd eventually come by and then she would have to face him. Wouldn't it be easier to do it over the phone?

She clicked answer.

"Carrie? Where have you been? I've been trying to call you for over an hour now."

"I've been busy dealing with your girlfriend."

"Excuse me?"

"Rita something or other. She stopped by to tell me to stop seeing you. That you were hers. I wish you would have told me you were taken before we slept together."

"This is not what it seems, Carrie. That woman is a piranha."

Carrie cleared her clogged throat. "Did she become that before or after your lurid affair?"

"Can we talk about this in person, please? I need to explain what happened."

"I see no reason for that. Frankly, I'd just as soon not ever see your face again."

"Please, Carrie…"

She ended the call and burst into tears. That was the hardest thing she had ever done. She prayed that he'd heed her warning and stay away, otherwise she'd break into a million pieces if she had to see him again.

Chapter Twenty

Tate downed his third beer, not feeling any better than when he started his first. Sure, the alcohol was affecting him, yet his gut still hurt knowing Carrie didn't want to see him again. He was brokenhearted, crushed, not sure what to do to fix this with her, or if he ever could.

Just the thought of never seeing her again ended him, made him miserable.

He rose and tossed the bottle into the trash can and went to get another, the doorbell making him stop.

Carrie? Could she have changed her mind?

He darted to the front door and swung it open, only to find Rita standing there, dressed in a sleazy-looking red dress and matching three-inch heels. She smiled a seductive smile, one that soured Tate's stomach.

"What do you want?" He tried to keep his cool. Losing it wouldn't get him anywhere. She and her husband could make his life even harder if they wanted to. Then, he'd never get his career back on track.

"You're mad at me." She plastered on a smirk.

Keep your cool.

"I have nothing more to say to you, Rita. I told you to go back to your husband and I meant it."

"You and I both know why I don't want to do that. He isn't attracted to me. I'm simply a prop for him to hide his real interests—men."

"And, as you told me yourself, you knew that when you married him. This is your bed, Rita, you need to lie in it or leave the man."

Her amber eyes filled with tears, and she reached out to try and touch him. "But I love you."

Tate clenched his teeth and pushed her hand away. This woman had no idea what love was, and if he was being serious, he hadn't either until he'd met Carrie. The realization almost sent his knees buckling. He was in love with Carrie, and he had to do something to make her understand that.

"Look, Rita, I don't feel the same. I love someone else."

"You can't be serious? You're telling me you love that mousy little dog groomer?"

Her words broke his calm demeanor. There wasn't one thing about Carrie that was plain, or mousey. She was stunning in every way.

"Yes, I love Carrie, and you need to get that through your thick skull now. Go back to Washington. Get a divorce if that will make you happy, then find someone else to love. It's not going to be me."

He closed the door and walked back to the kitchen, reaching into the refrigerator for another beer. He'd wallow for the night, then he'd get back to work and give Carrie a few days to absorb everything while he found out who had access to this genetic testing company's data and if they could be linked to the hospital where the judge's wife had her heart transplant.

He took a long swallow of his beer, his mind spinning. He loved Carrie. Carrie loved Kendall. The only way to be with her was to change his plans. Not going back to Washington, D.C., meant not being close to his sister Mya. Not being able to watch his niece grow up. That alone would be hard to do. He needed a sounding board, someone to talk this through with. He glanced at the clock on the wall. It was eight o'clock here, which meant it was nine there. Mia could already be in bed.

He went to retrieve his phone, still unsure if he should call her. He thumbed through his contacts and found her details, staring at the number until it blurred. He sucked in some air and pressed call, not sure what he'd say if she answered.

"Big brother! It's about time you called me."

"Sorry about that. I've been busy working on a story."

"Anything you can share with me?"

"Not yet, but I promise to when it's ready for publication. How are you feeling?"

"I'm feeling well. Hit that nesting stage all the baby books talk about. I was going to call you tomorrow. We have some news."

"Oh, yeah? What's that?"

"Jordan came home tonight to tell me he's being transferred overseas to their London office. In three months, we will be on our way. I'm looking for housing as we speak."

Tate never expected to hear this, wasn't sure what to say. His baby sister was going to move thousands of miles away from him. Away from D.C.

"Are you okay with this?" he asked.

"I'd be lying if I told you I wasn't shocked by the news. But I can't be without my husband, and this is a huge opportunity for him. I need to support his decision."

"I understand that more than you know."

165

"What do you mean?" she asked.

Tate wasn't sure how to share with his sister, even though the two were as close as two people could be.

"I met someone. The feelings I have for her even shocked me."

"Please tell me it's not that Rita woman."

"What? No, of course not."

"Okay, then who is she?"

"You are probably not going to believe this, but she lives here in Kendall, and she's a dog groomer."

"She sounds fabulous. When am I going to meet her?"

"That's the thing. She's not speaking to me right now."

"Why is that?" his sister asked.

"Rita showed up here and told her what happened. She didn't take it well, something I knew and the reason I didn't tell her."

"I still can't believe you slept with that viper."

"You and me both. I blame the bottle of Patron and the crocodile tears she shed at the time. The woman is quite the little actress. I can just imagine what she said to Carrie."

"So, her name is Carrie? Do you love her?"

"I do. She's amazing, and smart. She could run circles around me."

"Good. You need someone who'll keep you on your toes."

"Yeah, I just hope I can get her to see I'm not a homewrecker. I'm sure she's thinking that right now." Tate had to make her see that, or this newfound love was going to die as fast as it came to life.

****

Carrie wiped her eyes. It had been two days since she'd seen Tate—two very miserable days. She'd spent most of that time crying, then kicking herself for crying. Her heart hurt, and it made her angry that she allowed him to affect her in this way.

With a deep sigh, she stepped into her garage, setting up for a client's dog. One that was new to her from Bailey. Hopefully, it'd keep her mind occupied for a few hours because her eyes were starting to get sore.

She grabbed her shampoo, conditioner and the large nail clippers. The dog was a chocolate lab named Choco, well-behaved according to the Neils.

A knock on the door had her turning to find Tate, an unsure look on his handsome face. God, the man was gorgeous. She should have realized he was above her weight class the first time she'd met him.

"What do you want?" She reached inside a wheeled cart for her dog brushes.

"I know you said you never wanted to see me again, but I need to talk to you."

"About what, Tate? I never dreamed you'd do what you did. I just can't be with someone like that."

"I need to explain why it happened and who Rita and John are. Please let me do that."

"How is that going to change anything?"

His amazing eyes softened. "Just give me a chance to try."

She glanced at her phone to see what time it was. Her client would be there at two. "You have fifteen minutes. I have work coming."

"Okay. I met Rita in the elevator on Capitol Hill. She was crying at the time. My mistake was asking why. She told me that she caught her husband having sex with

167

one of his aides. She pleaded with me to have a drink with her. I could blame too much alcohol, but I won't. I slept with her. It was stupid, and when I told her I didn't want to continue, she would cry and plead and I'd give in. Until we were finally caught, and I was run out of D.C. She, on the other hand, became the victim in the whole debauchery. People don't exactly like the media right now. Her husband's affairs were spoken of in hushed tones all around town, but I was the one to lose my job. I know that doesn't excuse what I did. I wanted to tell you, but I knew you wouldn't understand."

Carrie held her anger in check. "Why wouldn't you at least try? When Rita showed up at the door, she made it seem as if I was getting in the way of some plan the two of you had made. How was I supposed to take that?"

"I never made any plans with this woman. I never wanted to see her again. I finally realized something the other day. I'm not cutthroat enough for that town. Those people are all a bunch of jackals. One way to your face, another behind your back. I don't want that."

She stared at him, trying to determine if he was telling the truth or not. "But I thought that your plans were to return to Washington, go back to your career there. Wasn't that why you were working on the genetic testing story?"

"I wanted to go back because Mya is there. A few nights ago, I learned her husband is being transferred to London. There is no need for me to go back now."

Carrie's stomach made a deep nosedive. Did that mean he was moving to England? Miles and miles away. The thought alone was like a knife to the heart.

Another knock brought her back to the present. A tall, regal-looking lady with silver hair stood holding a leash with a rich brown lab on its end.

"I've got work to do, Tate."

He nodded, then turned to leave, petting the dog on the way out.

Carrie went into survival mode. She welcomed Mrs. Neil and then took the dog's reins and told the woman to come back in two hours to pick Choco up. She had a lot to think about, but work came first. If nothing else, she had to continue to support herself. She had a mortgage to pay and dwelling on her love life wasn't going to pay it.

She soothed the dog, who seemed a bit jumpy. Once she'd settled the dog, she managed to get her into the bath, connect the noose to keep the dog restrained and then retrieved the sprayer and wet the dog down. She grabbed the soap and worked it up in Choco's coat, the lavender scent calming her nerves.

After she was clean, she squeezed on a conditioner and worked it in the fur, leaving it on long enough to clip the dog's nails, then rinsing it off. While draining the tub, she grabbed the large towels.

As she was drying Choco off, her mind drifted back to Tate. Maybe she had been too hard on him. He wasn't the one who was married, and with the woman's husband being a serial adulterer, perhaps it wasn't quite as clear cut. One thing she did want to know was if he'd learned anything on the testing and the judge's wife. She had a vested interest in the story and where it'd led Tate. Once Mrs. Neil came to pick up her dog, she was going to locate the man in question and find out.

Chapter Twenty-One

Tate gave it his all. He couldn't do anything else. He told Carrie his side of things, now it was up to her whether she forgave him or not.

He drove down Main Street, his attention drawn to a pair of news vans parked in a lot next to the café where he'd planned to stop for coffee. What the hell was going on?

He hesitated a moment, then decided not to stop. He'd drive to Bailey and meet with the judge in the Chandler case. His clerk had called him late afternoon yesterday to set up a meeting and he'd spent the remainder of the night working up a series of questions to ask. He'd maneuver around what had happened to his wife. If he'd heard of the genetic testing company and if they provided DNA information to the hospital where his wife had her transplant. The man might very well be innocent, not know anything about it, but Tate was planning to go in thinking he did.

Before going to the courthouse, Tate parked in front of a small coffee shop and stepped inside, the aroma in the air intoxicating to his senses. He stepped to the counter, studying the options above the waitress. "I'll take a vanilla hazelnut coffee to go, please."

As he waited, he looked around, spotting a cardholder with Carrie's dog kennel and grooming cards. This had to be the coffee shop where she'd waited for him the day he'd met with Adler. Probably how Carrie had gotten her new business.

Outside, he took a sip of his coffee, then decided to walk across the street to the courthouse where he'd meet with the judge. His nerves were starting to get the better of him. He wished Carrie were here to give him a pep talk. She always managed to make him feel better, even just by being present.

He was screened at the door, the officer friendly and helpful. Down the long corridor, he started to sweat. What if the judge had known about how these organs were attained? Could he be putting himself in danger?

At the clerk's office, he smiled at the woman who'd taken an interest in him. "How are you today?" He tried to appear unfazed by what he was about to learn.

"I'm fine, thanks. Take a seat and I'll let the judge know you are here."

Tate did as instructed, while inwardly calming himself. He'd dealt with powerful people before. He could handle this.

The clerk's phone buzzed, and she answered, smiling over at him while she listened. "Okay," she said, then hung up the phone.

"The judge will see you now."

Tate rose. "Thank you."

Down the long hallway, his mind whirled. He had to handle this right, or he'd be out on his ass. Probably be blackballed again here in the state of Missouri. No way could he allow that to happen since he'd just come to the realization that he wasn't leaving. Carrie held his heart and going anywhere without her wasn't an option. He needed to be content working at *The Gazette*, doing small-town stories because this was her home, and he was staying put.

At the judge's door, he knocked and entered when asked to do so.

Tate walked to the man's massive oak desk, files and paper scattered on top. The man stood and reached out to shake his hand.

"Thanks for seeing me today, Judge. I know this is not a good time for you and I want to send my condolences to you and your family."

He nodded, his Adam's apple working up and down. He was clearly trying to show little to no emotion, something men of a certain age tended to do. "I appreciate your kind words. So, I have another meeting in a half hour, so we should get started. What exactly did you want to know about the Adler case?"

"First, I'm curious to know if the district attorney is working on trying to find his real killer?"

The question didn't faze the man. Not one flinch. "I really wouldn't be privy to that information. I assume they reopened the case."

Tate nodded. "I would imagine but they lost a lot of time with not investigating Adler's confession."

The judge shrugged. "Hardly their fault. They thought it was open and shut."

Tate studied the man closely. "Even after hearing about a similar murder a few miles away. I know that the sheriff of Kendall talked to the coroner here in town. They surely had their doubt then, right?"

"I don't have an answer for you. Sorry."

"So, what about the genetic testing kits that were found at both murder victims' homes? Did they follow up on that?"

The man's eyes narrowed. "I have no idea what you

are talking about. How would you know that?"

"Crime scene photos." Tate was walking a thin line telling him this, but he didn't know if the judge was involved with this testing company or not.

"How were you able to attain photos of the Tripp murder? Those are kept confidential."

"Sorry, that's a protected source." At all costs, he needed to shield himself. He didn't want to end up behind bars. Then he'd never be able to fix things with Carrie.

The judge studied Tate closely, the attention causing sweat to form in the hollow of his back.

"All right. So, any more questions?"

Tate had to ask this question—one that could cause things to get ugly real fast.

"Do you know where your wife's transplanted organ came from?"

The man's hazel eyes narrowed. "Why would you ask me that?"

"Does Holy Trinity Hospital deal with Family Genetics?"

The judge sat up straight. "I have no idea. What are you suggesting here, Mr. Donnelly?"

"It might be wise to ask, Judge."

"Are you telling me that her donated heart could have come from Vincent Tripp?"

"I think it's possible and something we need to find out. According to people in the know from the man's hometown, that man was a heavy drinker and might not have been in the best shape to be a donor if indeed he was."

Anger crossed the judge's features. "So, you are telling me that the heart Cathleen received could have been the reason she didn't survive?"

"I can't tell you that, sir, but you may want to consult the hospital on this. I have no way of doing that. No one would consider talking to me since I'm a reporter."

"Let me ask you a question?" the judge asked, then blew out a labored breath.

"Sure."

"When you came here today, did you think I knew about this?"

There was no reason for Tate to lie. He now believed the judge was innocent in all of this. "I wasn't sure. I came here to find out and I did."

"When did you start to think I was possibly involved?"

Again, there was no reason not to tell him the truth. "When I learned your wife had a heart transplant."

"How would you handle this?"

"How long was your wife on the transplant list? I'm wondering why she was chosen to receive an organ. Was her heart failing?"

"She'd only been on it six months. We were told it could be years before she would be considered. I wish I would have asked more questions."

"Then how were you contacted," Tate asked. He had so many questions. There had to be some reason that the judge's wife was picked above so many others.

"Dr. Carrara and I are members of the Raintree Golf Club. It's pretty exclusive. We have played golf together. Our wives are on the hospital's charity foundation. Have done several fundraisers together. We're close friends."

"I see." Could it be that simple? The doctor had chosen her because of his wife's friendship with his own? "What I suggest you do, judge, is ask the doctor if the hospital has a contract with Family Genetics, or the company does its DNA testing there. It's very possible that the doctor doesn't even know where the heart came from. But we need to know that. Until we do, we have to consider him as part of a black market for organs, and you and I both know how illegal that is."

****

Carrie's business was on a roll. She'd been busy all day and still had another grooming to do in an hour, just enough time to run to the coffee shop and grab her favorite brew. She could afford a cup after all her clients that day. Clearly, with Doug gone, and her being cleared of his murder, everyone and their dogs had returned. At this rate, she'd be able to afford all the new equipment upgrades she'd always wanted and then some. Maybe she'd even splurge on one of those fancy coffeemakers. Just the thought brought a smile to her face.

She quickly locked up and jumped in her truck, thinking of getting a Danish as well. She could use a rush of sugar before Princess showed up.

At the café, she was lucky to find a parking spot next to the door. She got out and stepped inside, a delicious aroma making her stomach growl. That was a yes on the Danish.

At the counter, she quickly ordered and stepped back to wait. As she was paying, Ted Alexander, one of the warehouse crew at the hardware store came up to her. "Hey, Carrie. I was wondering if you were free Friday night. There's a dance over at the VFW hall. I'd love to take you."

Carrie was instantly taken aback. All this time in Kendall and not one invitation until now. Was it because

Doug died and was no longer a threat? Did it really matter? Too bad she only had eyes for one man, and he'd disappointed her. Perhaps going out with someone else could clarify her feelings. Maybe this was all because of no one else taking a chance on getting to know her. She deserved an opportunity to find out. "That sounds like fun. How about I meet you there?" This way if she didn't feel right about it, she could leave.

"That'd be super. I'll see you there."

Carrie retrieved her coffee and Danish and left, heading back home. How many others would reach out to her now that Doug was no longer pulling the strings? The whole thing was infuriating to say the least. All these years of being alone and lonely all because of some man's sick obsession with her. That *it* wasn't something about her. Those days were over and done with now. She might have a social life as long as she could get past her feelings for Tate.

Back at her house, she scarfed down the Danish, while getting things set up for Princess. The dog was the reason she'd met Tate, the memory of that day coming back. He'd been such an ass that first encounter, though in his defense, he'd been attacked by the dog in his nether regions. She could understand his anger. Even that hadn't stopped him from coming to her aid when she needed it. Tate was a good man. She believed that in her heart. He'd made a mistake in D.C., sure, but who hadn't done something they regretted?

Was she willing to give him another chance? That was the million-dollar question, one she'd need time to think about. Maybe going on that date with Ted and seeing how it felt—noting if there was a spark of anything.

She took a sip of coffee. She still had fifteen minutes to enjoy her brew before Princess arrived.

Her phone chirped that she'd received a message. She grabbed it from her jacket and looked to see who it was from. Tate. Should she even look at it? Did she really want to be drawn into whatever he wanted to tell her? Then again, they'd been working on something important together. Could she pass on knowing if that was indeed what he was texting about?

She started to pace. Should she look at it or not?

No. Not right now. Carrie had a client coming. She needed to focus on that.

She quickly finished her coffee, then tossed the paper cup in the trash. As she was sharpening her shears, Princess and her owner bounded through the door, the woman holding the leash looking frazzled. Carrie couldn't blame her. Princess was a big dog and young and healthy. A lethal combination.

"How's my beautiful girl doing?" she asked, ruffling the dog's fur around her fluffy neck. She wiggled and rubbed up against Carrie, clearly happy to see her.

"I'll pick her up in an hour and a half." Mrs. Grenell looked for an affirmative from Carrie.

"I should be done by then, yes."

Carrie watched her leave, then went to work. At least until she was done with Princess, she wouldn't be dwelling on Tate and what he had to tell her, and that was a good thing.

Chapter Twenty-Two

Tate heard the doorbell ring and instantly thought of Carrie again. The woman was always on his mind. She'd wrapped herself around his heart and all he could think about was holding her in his arms, loving her the way he had.

He rushed to answer, the happy bubble bursting when it was Rita instead.

"What do you want?" Tate wasn't sure he could keep his cool this time. She'd become obsessed with him, and he was tired of it.

"I wanted to warn you that John's in town. He flew into Kansas City last night and drove here this morning. I'm afraid he is going to try to confront you." She reached out to touch him.

Tate shoved her hand away. "Let him!" Tate thought that would be the only way to get rid of them both. Her husband needed to know where Tate stood. He had to be told he didn't want anything to do with Rita. Maybe Mr. Philips would be able to talk some sense into his wife.

"Why are you being like this? I told you I love you. Doesn't that matter?"

"And I told you, I love Carrie. I just want you to leave me alone."

Her amber eyes filled with tears. "Please, Tate. Let me in and we can talk."

"I'm sorry but I have to go. I'm working on a story.

I don't have time for this. Go tell your husband to go back to Washington and leave me alone."

Tate then closed the door and went to round up his things to leave. He was going to Family Genetic to talk to someone there, see how their tests are reviewed and where the data is stored—who had excess to their DNA results.

He grabbed his computer bag, a mug filled with coffee for the ride, and his keys.

At the door he willed Rita to be gone. Outside, he was relieved when she wasn't anywhere in sight.

He walked to his vehicle and was unlocking the door when a male voice stopped him. He turned and was blindsided by a fist to his right cheek, the impact making him bounce off his Jeep. Only sheer will kept him from going down.

"Stay the fuck away from my wife," the congressman said, his eyes narrowed, his lips thinned into a harsh, straight line.

Tate rubbed his face, becoming angrier than he'd ever been in his life. "You need to tell Rita that since I already explained to her that I don't want her here."

The man seemed to be contemplating what Tate told him. "What are you saying?"

"I'm saying that I told your wife I love someone else and she's having a hard time hearing what I'm saying. Maybe you can get through to her. I can't seem to do that."

"Why would she come here if you haven't led her on?"

"I blocked her on my phone the last time she tried to contact me. Look, Congressman, I have no intention of seeing your wife again. Take her home, get your act together, tell her the truth, I don't care, I just want both of you to leave me alone. As of a few days ago, I've decided I'm staying here in Kendall. I have no interest in being at the Capitol any longer. I just want to get on with my life."

"Don't you have a sister living in D.C.?"

"I do, but her and her husband are moving to London for his job. I'm staying here."

The man stepped back and stuffed his hands in the pockets of his trousers.

When he remained silent, Tate opened his Jeep door. "You might want to tell the truth about who you are. Let Rita move on. Maybe then, you both could be happy."

Tate jumped into the seat and closed the door. He wasn't going to kick a dead horse. Either the man stepped out of the closet, or he didn't. Tate didn't care as long as he and Rita left Kendall and never came back.

On the road, he took a sip of his coffee, still waiting for an answer from Carrie on the text he'd sent her earlier that day. He was starting to think she wasn't planning to forgive him. At least, she could ask how his story was panning out. She'd seemed really excited about helping him. Could she shut that all down because of his indiscretion? Wouldn't she want to know if the judge was involved? If the roles were reversed, he certainly would.

As he entered the city, his phone beeped. Hopefully it was Carrie. He drove down Main Street and out to the warehouse district where the testing company was located. He had no idea why he hadn't done this sooner since both murder victims had the testing kit in their homes. They'd clearly used the service.

He finally found the office, strangely way back in

the back of a row of rundown buildings. That alone seemed shady as shit.

Tate reached for his phone, finding a message from Carrie.

—I'm busy. What did you want?—

—Checking out the genetic testing facility in Bailey. Would like to talk when I get back—

He sent the text and tucked the phone in his jacket pocket, then got out and started for the front door.

Inside was as drab as the outside, not what he expected for sure. There was a glass partisan that looked grimy, so unlike any medical facility he'd ever seen before. Something was wrong with this picture and a ball of dread worked its way into his stomach. Maybe he should leave. Call the sheriff and have him check the place out instead.

Then again, would the man even take him seriously? Probably not. Best to get through this, see if anyone was around and hope for the best.

A big man with a long, unkempt beard stepped out a door and frowned at him. "Are you here for the liver?" the man asked.

"No." Tate became even more concerned by the question. "I came to find out more information about your services."

"The doctor isn't around. You'll need to come back some other time."

"You don't have a pamphlet or something I could take to read?"

The door behind him squeaked open and in stepped a heavyset man in a white coat; on his chubby face were a pair of thick glasses perched on a huge, bulbous nose. "Doc. This guy wants to talk to you about our services."

The man's dark, beady eyes narrowed. "What do you want to know?"

"I was just wondering if you send a kit out and then I send it back? Do you email the results or send it regular mail?"

"Why are you inquiring? What are you needing to know?"

"Family history. I lost my father when I was young. I'd like to find out if I'm predisposed to any diseases. I have no way of finding that out without a DNA screening."

The man nodded. "I see. I'd be glad to show you around, give you some literature and then you can decide how in-depth you want to go. Follow me and we'll get started." He turned to the other man. "Take care of that issue and then join me in the lab."

For whatever reason, something didn't feel right, and he wasn't sure he should go anywhere with this doctor. Though, how could he back out now?

He cleared his throat and followed the man through the door they had stepped out from and walked down a long hallway and into a room that was much cleaner than the rest of the place. Off to the right was another area that was covered in clear plastic, appearing somewhat like a medical facility, with a long steel table and what looked like monitoring equipment for doing surgeries. He turned back to the doctor, who was watching him intently.

"So, what did you say your name was?" the doctor asked.

"I didn't say. My name is Tate. And you are?"

"Dr. Fanta."

Tate shifted from one foot to the other, his nerves

trying to get the better of him. Yet, he needed to stay calm and cool. Otherwise, the doctor was going to get suspicious.

"Can I get that literature? I have somewhere to be in an hour."

"Of course." He turned and stepped into an office off to the right of that makeshift surgery and then a few moments later returned with a box and a pamphlet.

Exactly like the boxes in Tripp's and Mr. Chandler's homes. There was something off with this man and his testing facility. If Tate had to wager a guess, the guy had lured both victims here, drugged them, and removed their organs, then the goon out front returned them to their homes undetected. His only question was if the hospital receiving the organs was involved. That's what he needed to find out.

"Are you affiliated with any of the hospitals in the area?" Tate took a risk by asking but he needed to know.

"We do business all over the state."

That was vague as hell. Was there a reason for that? Tate would love to know but if he pried too much, he'd give himself away, and then who knew what could happen. Two men were already dead. He was sure they'd have no qualms at adding him to that death toll, not that there couldn't be more. Just because no other bodies were discovered with no organs didn't mean anything. They could be missing persons, buried somewhere. There was a realm of possibilities. Unfortunately, to find that out, he'd be endangering his own life.

The doctor handed him the box with the pamphlet on top.

"Thank you. I appreciate your time. Can you tell me how long it takes from when you receive my DNA to results being sent?"

"A week to ten days usually. It depends on how many we're analyzing at the time. It's been a bit slow around here, so it shouldn't be more than a week."

Tate nodded. "Okay then. I appreciate your answering my questions."

"Can I show myself out?" Tate wanted nothing more than to get the hell out of there. Bad images were starting to take shape in his mind. So, the sooner he left, the better.

"Go ahead. I look forward to receiving your sample."

Tate smiled, then walked to the door, the hair on his neck still wreaking havoc on his nervous system. He pushed the door open and stepped into the hall. A pain shot through him, then everything went black.

****

Carrie checked her phone for the fifth time in the last two hours, pacing the floor, a sick feeling forming in the pit of her stomach. It'd been six hours since Tate had texted her telling her where he was and that he wanted to talk when he returned. Way too long for something not to be wrong. She knew it. But what could she do? Go find this testing facility? What if they had done something to Tate? She wouldn't fare any better. No, she was going to have to go to the sheriff and hope he took her seriously.

With that, she quickly took Molly out, not knowing when she'd be able to get back. Once the dog relieved herself, Carrie raced to her truck, another half hour going by. She knew time could be running out if she didn't find him. Vince and that other man were dead, possibly because of those people at the facility. Just the thought of Tate meeting that same fate made her ill. She cared so much for him, even with what he'd done. If he made it through this, she was going to give him another chance. Tell him how much he meant to her, even if he planned to leave soon. They could spend that remaining time together.

In front of the police station, she jumped out of her truck and raced inside, finding her friend sitting behind the desk. "Is the sheriff around? I need to talk to him now."

"What's going on?" Emily asked, looking concerned. "Have the Walshes been bugging you again?"

"No. Tate's missing. He went to investigate something over in Bailey and he never returned. I need the sheriff to look into it. I'm afraid something bad has happened."

"Let me run and get him. I'll be right back." Her friend got up and sped down the hallway and stepped into the man's office. Only moments later, the two returned, the sheriff taking the lead.

"When was the last time you talked to Mr. Donnelly?"

"It's been almost seven hours. He texted me that he was at a genetic testing facility, checking out a lead, said he'd get back to me, but I haven't heard a word. That's not like him. I'm worried."

"What kind of lead was he following?"

"Both the dead men who were missing organs had a kit from this company in their homes. That seemed odd to him, and he went to follow that up."

"Do you know where this facility is?"

"Only that it's in Bailey."

"I'll ride over there and see what I can find out."

"Let me go with you. I need to know he's okay."

He looked like he wanted to say no but nodded instead. "Emily, find out their address and radio me when you have it."

"Okay, Sheriff."

"Come on," he said to Carrie. "Seven hours is a long time. Anything could have happened by now."

He was right. Why had she waited so long to contact him? If anything had happened to Tate, it was her fault for not realizing this sooner.

It took thirty-five minutes to get to Bailey, another twenty to find the facility, strangely in the warehouse district. On the very end. When they parked, they saw no sign of Tate's Jeep anywhere. "You stay here. I'm going to go in and see if anyone spoke to Donnelly."

"Are you sure you don't want me to go with you?" Carrie had a bad feeling about him going in alone.

He shook his head. "Emily would have my hide if I let anything happen to you. Stay put. I'll be back in a moment or two."

She rubbed the back of her neck and watched him step inside the dirty glass door, thinking the place couldn't be right. Who would ever do business with a service that worked out of such an unsightly place?

Each minute that ticked by made her nerves tingle. She couldn't sit here and do nothing. She'd walk around, see if that didn't help her calm down. She took off toward the back of the metal building, her eyes instantly connecting with Tate's Jeep hidden in the back. He was here. Inside. And so was the sheriff. How long had they been here? Was he in trouble now?

She raced back to the police car and picked up the

radio, praying that both men were still alive. "Emily," she called through the mic.

"What's the matter?" Emily asked.

"We need the local cops here now."

"I'm calling them as we speak. Hang on."

"I can't. I have to go in and make sure the sheriff and Tate are okay."

"No, Carrie. Don't do that. Wait for backup."

"I can't. I need to see if I can help."

"How? Do you have a weapon?"

Her best friend had a point but how could she hold back when lives were at stake.

Carrie was going to try and sneak in and hope no one noticed.

She eased the door open slowly, on alert for anyone. She made it to another door when she heard feet shuffling from on the other side. She held back, hoping to hear the sheriff's voice. Seconds ticked into minutes until she couldn't in all conscience wait any longer.

She turned the knob on the door, peeking inside, finding a long hallway, no one around. She stepped in and gently closed the door. No one knew the sheriff had not come alone. That was the one thing she had going for her.

At the end of the corridor were two other doors, one to the left, the other to the right. Which one should she open? Should she flip a coin? *Keep it together and just pick one.*

She opened the one to the right, plying the door open slowly, voices stopping her from going in. "We need to get the fuck out of here. Everything has gone to shit all because you got sloppy and forgot those goddamned test kits. Now, we are going to have to leave the country."

"What are we going to do with them?"

"What do you think? They know who we are. You are going to have to take care of them."

"Why me? Why don't you do it? I'm tired of doing all the dirty work."

"Are you serious? I've done all the harvesting of organs. I'm the brains in this operation. You're the muscle. Now, use that muscle and take care of them."

Carrie's jaw dropped. She had to do something now. She couldn't let anything happen to either the sheriff or Tate. She needed to create a distraction until the local police arrived. But what kind?

She could pretend to be a customer. Carrie backtracked to the front office, noticing a button to push for service. She pressed it, hoping that both men would come. At least then she'd know the other wasn't harming Tate or the sheriff.

Okay. When they came, what was she going to say? All she needed to do was stall them until the cops arrived.

A short, heavyset man stepped out of the door. *Dammit.* Why couldn't it have been both?

"Can I help you?"

"I was hoping you could give me a little information on your testing services," she said, her voice a bit shaky. She prayed that the man didn't notice.

"I'm sorry but we are in the process of closing our service. We weren't getting enough business."

"I see. Could you possibly recommend someone else in the field?"

"No. Not offhand."

This wasn't working and who knew what was happening in the back. The other guy could be killing them as she spoke.

Suddenly, sirens blared in the distance and the man's eyes widened. He tried to grab for her but she sidestepped him and raced inside the door. Carrie had to help Tate and the sheriff. She raced to the back, surprised not to be followed. Then again, the creep was probably trying to escape.

She pushed open the other door and came through, shocked to see that both the sheriff and Tate had tackled the other man to the ground and had him restrained.

Relief had her body release the tension she'd been holding inside. Only moments later, police came through the door and went to help the man up and took control.

Tate came over to her and pulled her into his arms. "Thank you for being concerned about me. I'd be dead now if it wasn't for you and the sheriff."

"I was worried when you didn't text or call. I knew something wasn't right."

"Why don't you two go on home," the sheriff said, coming up to them. "I'll hang around and see if we can find evidence to prove these two killed Vincent or any others."

Carrie nodded and followed Tate out of the building. "Your Jeep's in the back. I found it when I was searching for another way inside."

They walked around the building. "Can you drive?" he asked, looking at her. "I got a nice crack to the noggin and I'm still seeing double."

"Should I take you to the hospital?"

He shook his head. "I'll be fine, and if I'm not, I'll see Doc Havers. According to the sheriff, they allow walk-ins."

Carrie couldn't help but smile. "Yes, he does."

On the drive back to Kendall, Tate was surprisingly

quiet, so unlike the man. "Are you all right?" she asked, glancing over at him.

"I just have a lot on my mind."

"Care to share?"

"I'm not sure you're ready to hear it just yet."

She didn't know what to say to that. Maybe he was going to tell her he was moving to London to be with his sister. How would she deal with that? Perhaps this was a good time to tell him how she felt? Maybe he needed an alternative? But this didn't seem like the right time. She'd give him a day to recover first. Then she'd tell him how she felt and hope he wanted the same thing.

Chapter Twenty-Three

Tate woke and rolled to his side, wishing Carrie was there lying next to him. He'd wanted to tell her that he planned to stay in town and work hard to earn her trust again, but his head was pounding, and he didn't think it was the best time. Today, if he could get her alone, he'd tell her. He just hoped she'd give him that chance.

He rose and went to shower, thinking that he'd go back and see if the sheriff was able to find out how many possible people were involved in this whole genetic testing scam. If certain hospitals were implicated as well.

On the way to the police station, he stopped to get some coffee, running into Emily who was waiting at the counter. "Hey, is the sheriff at the station? I wanted to stop in and talk to him."

"He is. I've heard he has a lot to tell you. Have you talked to Carrie this morning?" she asked.

"I haven't. I wanted to see the sheriff first. Is everything okay?"

"As far as I know it is. She told me you two had some problem, but she never went into what."

"You might as well know that I had a sordid affair with a married woman in D.C. It's why I left. She came here looking for me. Then her husband arrived. I hope they packed up and left town yesterday."

"Is that affair over?" Emily asked.

"Yes, before I left D.C. But this lady didn't

understand that."

"And Carrie knows all about this?"

"Everything but the woman's husband being in town. He showed up right before I left for Bailey. I told him to take his wife and leave. To never come back."

"Here is your order, Emily?" the waitress behind the counter said.

"I'll see you at the station," she said, then turned to leave.

Tate ordered a coffee, paid her, and left himself, wanting to get this story straight so he could go and work things out with Carrie. He'd make her love him if it took a lifetime to accomplish. He wasn't going anywhere. She'd changed his life, made him see that work wasn't enough to keep him fulfilled. He needed so much more. Mya had realized that when she met her husband. Tate understood that now.

He drove into a slot in front of the police station and parked. For whatever reason, what he learned from the sheriff was going to be dark and sordid, not unlike D.C. politics. Why hadn't he seen that before? From now on, he was going to be content writing about water main breaks and new business openings, and hopefully an occasional juicy story to help with the monotony.

Inside, he found an older couple sitting in the waiting area, both looking as grim as any people he'd ever seen. He wondered why.

He turned as Emily stepped out of the sheriff's office, the sheriff following directly behind him. He motioned a nod to Tate, then turned to the couple. "Mr. and Mrs. Tripp, can you come with me." Vince's parents. They were about to learn that their son was murdered because of his DNA. This was going to be a shock. Hell, the whole thing was crazy to him, and he'd lived in D.C. for years. That city was as bizarre as they came.

He went and sat where the couple had just left and took out his phone. He'd text Carrie and see if they couldn't meet for lunch to talk. He pressed send and sat back to wait. Emily had gone back in with the sheriff, probably to help comfort Mrs. Tripp. He wouldn't want to have to do that. Ten minutes passed and still no text from Carrie. Did that mean she didn't want to talk to him? Or was she busy?

If it wasn't for her, he might be dead right now and he wanted to thank her for going to the sheriff. Then, she'd even risked her own life to get to him. He'd never forget that.

The Tripps reemerged from the office, Mrs. Tripp dabbing at her tear-filled eyes, looking sad. He couldn't blame her. Even though the man had his vices, he didn't deserve to die. All because he was a match to someone considered worthier than him. At least that was what Tate assumed.

The sheriff came to the waiting area and smiled at Tate. "You wanted to see me?"

"I wondered if you have a few minutes."

"I think I could squeeze you in. Come into my office."

Tate rose and smiled at Emily, who they passed on the way.

Inside, Tate took a seat, thinking about what he really wanted to know today. There was time to pull all the information together for his exposé but right now he just wanted to know how many innocent people could have been murdered.

"I first want to thank you again for what you helped

uncover, Tate. I don't know how you got the crime scene photos for the Tripp murder, and I don't want to know. I'm just thankful you put two and two together."

"Have you gotten ahold of Dr. Fanta's files to see how many DNA matches were made and if anyone was killed to get them?"

"I have my deputies going through them right now. Organs were given to three recipients at Trinity—the judge's wife you told me about yesterday, also a CEO of an insurance agency just placed on the donor list and a rich woman who was denied because she's an alcoholic. We are working on getting their bank records to see if money changed hands."

"Are they still alive since the transplants?"

"Yes."

"So, why didn't the judge's wife survive?"

"Early this morning, I talked to the woman's doctor. He told me her body had been so weak that she couldn't fight off an infection she got. They weren't sure if it was rejection or not. We do know that the judge didn't pay for the heart she received."

Tate frowned. "So, it wasn't the heart that caused her death?"

"They are doing an autopsy right now on her. We should know by tomorrow morning."

"Have you talked to anyone at the FBI to see if these two goons had been doing this anywhere else?"

"I'm waiting for someone there to call me back. That's up in the air right now. I will let you know when I learn anything. I have a question for you, Donnelly."

"Oh, yeah, what's that?" Tate asked.

"What do you plan on doing when this story breaks? Are you going back to D.C.?"

"Actually, I'm planning to stay here. I have a personal story to put an ending on, one with a certain redhead."

The sheriff smiled. "You don't say? I'm sure she'll be receptive to that."

"I hope you're right." He rose from his seat. "You'll let me know when you learn something?"

"I will. You do the same. Carrie's a good woman. You'd be lucky to have her."

Tate sighed. "That, I know. I just hope she feels the same."

****

Carrie held the leash tight while Princess dragged her down the sidewalk. She tried to reel her in, but the animal was too strong. Why did this feel like a déjà vu moment?

Princess shot sideways and Carrie lost her grip, the leash sliding through her fingers. The dog raced down the sidewalk toward a figure who had just turned onto the street in front of her house. She stared for a long, agonizing minute, not sure what to do.

With a frustrated breath, she raced after the animal, praying that she wouldn't knock the person on the sidewalk down.

When she got closer, her eyes widened, shocked that it was Tate the dog was now jumping on. *Oh, God.* How could this be happening? Same dog. Same guy. Only difference was she knew and loved the man Princess was attacking—not quite attacking, more loving on in Carrie's eyes.

She reached the dog and grabbed the leash, pulling her back. "You know this animal has an unrequited love for me," Tate said in a tone that was hard to gauge. "But

I want to know if you share those feelings."

She glanced up at his face, surprised by what he'd asked. There was a clear emotion radiating from him. He wanted to know how she felt.

"Before you answer, can I tell you something?"

"Okay," she said, unsure what could be said that would change the fact that he'd be leaving soon.

He held the dog in front of him and looked to be struggling with what he was going to tell her.

"Just say it, Tate. You're leaving. I knew this was your plan. I can't expect anything different."

"That's not what I was going to tell you. Actually, the opposite. I came here to say that I love you, Carrie, and I plan on staying in Kendall permanently. But if you want us to ever have children, you need to get this dog away from my babymakers."

Carrie wasn't sure if she should laugh or cry. It was funny that he referred to his package as such, yet he just changed her life in a matter of seconds.

After a long, frustrated sigh, she reeled the dog in close to her. Was she imagining all this or was he wanting a future with her?

"Are you trying to let me down easy by not saying anything?"

"But I thought you wanted to be with your sister?"

"She and her husband are moving to England. That's too far away, and even if they were staying in Washington, I'd want to be here with you. I can't live without you, Carrie. I need to be with you. You changed me. Made me see what was important. I want you and I want us to have a family someday. Please tell me you feel the same way."

Tears filled her eyes. "Yes. I do. I will. Forever and

always."

He smiled, reaching for her only to have Princess lunge for him again. "I don't suppose you could put that beast up so we can have a proper hello?"

"Only if you promise to spend the night and not leave in the morning."

"I'll call in to work sick. Whatever you want me to do, Carrie. I'm at your disposal for the rest of our lives."

Carrie gave him a seductive up-and-down appraisal. "Let me just say, you are in trouble for the next fifty years."

A word about the author...

Jerri Drennen is an author of romantic suspense as well as paranormal and contemporary romance. Growing up on a farm in a tiny town in Minnesota was where she started reading romance and learned how to make up stories in her head. After meeting her husband, she moved to his hometown in Missouri where she now live with one of their four children. Her kids call her the crazy cat lady.

Thank you for purchasing
this publication of The Wild Rose Press, Inc.

For questions or more information
contact us at
info@thewildrosepress.com.

The Wild Rose Press, Inc.
www.thewildrosepress.com